P9-EAO-024

ISBN 978-0-316-30693-5

9 780316 306935

50799

EAN

Will the carnival be big enough for
the both of them?

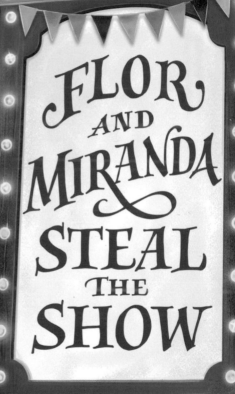

FLOR
AND
MIRANDA
STEAL
THE
SHOW

JENNIFER TORRES

Little, Brown and Company
Hachette Book Group
1290 Avenue of the Americas, New York, NY 10104
Visit us at LBYR.com

Originally published in hardcover and ebook by Little, Brown and Company in June 2018
First Trade Paperback Edition: June 2020

Little, Brown and Company is a division of Hachette Book Group, Inc. The Little, Brown name and logo are trademarks of Hachette Book Group, Inc.

The publisher is not responsible for websites (or their content) that are not owned by the publisher.

The Library of Congress has cataloged the hardcover edition as follows:
Names: Torres, Jennifer, 1980– author.
Title: Flor and Miranda steal the show / by Jennifer Torres.
Description: First Edition. | New York : Little, Brown and Company, 2018. | Summary: "When Flor finds out that Miranda and her band could potentially put her family's petting zoo out of business, she forms a plan to keep Miranda from an important performance that night"— Provided by publisher.
Identifiers: LCCN 2017020283| ISBN 9780316306898 (hardcover) | ISBN 9780316306911 (ebook) | ISBN 9780316306881 (library edition ebook)
Subjects: | CYAC: Carnivals—Fiction. | Bands (Music)—Fiction. | Petting zoos—Fiction. | Friendship—Fiction. | Hispanic Americans—Fiction.
Classification: LCC PZ7.1.T65 Flo 2018 | DDC [Fic]—dc23
LC record available at https://lccn.loc.gov/2017020283

ISBNs: 978-0-316-30693-5 (pbk.), 978-0-316-30691-1 (ebook)

Printed in the United States of America

LSC-C

Printing 3, 2022

FLOR AND MIRANDA STEAL THE SHOW

BY JENNIFER TORRES

LITTLE, BROWN AND COMPANY
New York Boston

FOR MY GRANDPARENTS:
MARY AND VALDEMAR ESPINOZA,
JOSEPHINE AND SAMUEL TORRES

Flor

(12:05 P.M.—SHOWTIME)

It didn't matter whether we were in Visalia or Ventura, whether it was one hundred degrees out on some baked-grass fairgrounds in the valley or cool and foggy on the coast. It could be Friday, it could be Saturday, it could be Sunday. Did not matter: She was never more than three songs into the show before someone in the audience stood up and danced. *Never.*

Miranda y los Reyes. There were three of them. A boy with a guitar, a girl with an accordion, and Miranda. She was the one with the microphone.

They wore matching cowboy hats and blue jean vests with silver studs around the collar. I saw them for the first time back in June, at the Kern County Fair. Local talent, same as we had wherever we went. Hometown acts always helped drum up a crowd. Only, Miranda y los Reyes brought in such a *big* crowd that Mr. Barsetti—he was in charge—said to their dad, "Have you ever thought about going full-time on the carnival circuit? Why don't you come along with us for the summer, see how it goes?"

And, just like that, they did. Like all along they knew he would ask and knew they'd say yes. Like they were already packed up and ready to hit the road.

At least that's how Lexanne from the frozen lemonade booth said it happened. And lucky thing for Mr. Barsetti, since the Baker Brothers and their Marionette Theater had just retired and moved away to Arizona, and he needed someone to take over the noon show on the Family Side Stage.

I never missed the noon show, and I can tell you, Miranda y los Reyes had not changed their act all summer. Not by one single note. It started with a couple of slow-swaying love songs, like the kind Grandpa used to listen to while he worked on the truck.

But after that, it was like all of a sudden, they would wake up. The older girl, the sister, she would shout, "¡Uno! Dos! Tres!" She would stretch open her accordion, and her fingers would fly over those little white buttons. Then she'd sort of nod at the brother, and he would start playing too: *thrum, thrum, thrum, thrum*. Only *fast*.

Miranda would close her eyes and lean in toward the

microphone. She would tap out the rhythm, first with the toe of her boot, then with her hand against the side of her leg, until finally, she would open her eyes and she'd sing.

She was small. Smaller than me, anyway, but she had a voice like fireworks bursting, raining glittery flecks of light all over the audience. And wherever they fell, someone got up and danced. It was like magic had hit them.

To tell the truth, I missed the marionettes.

Miranda y los Reyes wasn't a bad show. The thing of it was, I did not go to the Family Side Stage for the show.

I went because noon was the only time I knew for sure that Papá didn't need me at the petting zoo. And the Family Side Stage was the only place I knew for sure I could find some peace and a spot to sit in the shade.

Fairgrounds after fairgrounds, up and down the state, no one went to the Family Side Stage for the show. It was where they parked Grandma and the baby while everyone else got in line for the Turbo Drop. It was where they rested their feet and argued over what kind of food on a stick to buy for lunch. You could always find a few empty seats at the Family Side Stage.

But not lately.

That Sunday in August, the last day of the Dinuba Cantaloupe Fair, the only seat left was a metal folding chair right in the middle of the last row. I sighed. If I hadn't stopped for kettle corn, I might have found a better spot, somewhere on the aisle where no one would have noticed me coming or going. I would have to remember that next weekend, I told myself. All I could do in the meantime was try to get to the chair as quickly as I could, holding the bag over my head so popcorn wouldn't spill into anyone's lap. "Sorry," I whispered as I squeezed past knees and stepped cautiously over toes. "Excuse me."

The chair squeaked loudly as I settled into it. I cringed and looked around, but no one seemed to have heard. They were all too busy watching Miranda y los Reyes, which had just started its third song.

Someone in the audience whistled.

Someone stood and clapped.

Everything was right on schedule. Like I said, the show had not changed by a single note. There would be dancing any second.

Instead, the kid sitting in front of me howled. *Great.* There were always crying kids at the carnival, especially in the afternoon when they should have been home taking their naps. I could not stand crying.

The mom patted the kid's head—"Shhh"—but kept her eyes on the stage, craning her neck for a better view. "Shhh," she said again, "let's settle down now, Gracie. Mama wants to listen."

But Gracie did not settle down. She stood on her chair and started waving a big yellow balloon animal. What used to be a balloon animal, anyway. By then it was just a sad, lumpy tube. A yellow balloon *snake* if you were a glass-half-full kind of person, which this kid definitely was not.

She smacked me on the nose with it.

The mom spun around. "I am so sorry! Are you okay?" She took the balloon away. "Gracie, that's *enough*."

Gracie hollered even louder.

Give it back, give it back, I thought. *Anything to stop the crying.*

As if she could hear my thoughts, the mother gave the balloon right back. Maybe she couldn't stand the crying either. "All right, all right. Just . . . settle down. Please."

Smack. This time on my forehead. So much for settling down. So much for *peace.*

That was about as much as I could take. I had seen enough screaming kids at the petting zoo to know there was really only one way to deal with the situation. I set the kettle corn down between my feet, shook the crumbs off my hands, and reached over to tug gently on the little girl's wisp of a ponytail. She turned, and I pointed at the balloon.

"Can I see it?"

She looked at me, looked at the balloon, and shook her head.

"Come on, just for a sec? I want to show you something." She hugged the balloon to her chest, but she was curious, I could tell. She didn't take her eyes off me. "I will give it right back. Promise."

Finally, Gracie stretched out her arm, all covered in temporary tattoos, half peeling off, and laid the balloon in my open hand.

Before she could change her mind, I grabbed it, folded one end over the other, and twisted.

Gracie gasped. "No!"

"Shhh," her mom said.

I held up a finger. "Just wait. You'll like it."

Gracie gulped down her doubt. There wasn't much else she could do. I had her balloon, after all. But as each twist revealed ears! A nose! A tail! She smiled and squealed and finally calmed down.

I mean, I was no expert—I couldn't twist an octopus or an elephant or anything fancy like that—but I had spent enough time with Cordelia Cornflower, the Roller-Skating Balloon Fairy, to learn the basics.

"Here you go."

Then, just as I was handing Gracie her good-as-new yellow poodle, the audience roared.

For a split second, it seemed like the applause was for me, but that was impossible. The poodle was all right, but it wasn't *that* good.

Up onstage, where Gracie's mom was pointing, the girl with the accordion and the boy with the guitar were still playing. But Miranda wasn't with them anymore.

She had hopped down and started dancing with the audience. *That's new*, I thought.

"That's new," a voice behind me echoed, loud and a little surprised. "What is she doing? We never rehearsed this."

I looked over my shoulder. Mr. Barsetti was standing a few feet behind me with another man. The guy's hat and eyebrows told me he was with the Reyes family. The dad, if I had to guess. He crossed his arms over his chest.

"She's a natural performer, really knows how to work a crowd," Mr. Barsetti said. "I hope you've been happy here at Barsetti and Son All-American Extravaganzas, Reyes. Those kids of yours have a real future."

Mr. Barsetti was the son in Barsetti & Son, and we all worked for him at All-American Extravaganzas, a traveling carnival. Towns would hire us to put on their fairs, and our caravan would come rolling in with just about everything they needed: rides and games, food and entertainment. Plus the petting zoo, of course.

"They have a future, but it isn't on the side stage," Mr. Reyes said. "You can't keep her here forever, Barsetti. That girl is main-stage material. You can't tell me she's not. Look at this crowd. On a Sunday! If it wasn't for Miranda, this place would be empty. I know it, and you know it."

Mr. Barsetti crossed his arms too and said, "Hrrrmmm."

Mr. Reyes took off his hat and fanned himself with it. "All

we're asking for is a chance. Listen, I hear you need an opening act for tonight's main-stage show. The band you booked got sick?"

Mr. Barsetti made a noise like a growl that got stuck in his throat. "Stomach trouble."

So the rumors were true. It was the pickles. Had to have been the pickles. No one liked to admit it, but there were some foods you just shouldn't deep fry.

"So put Miranda on."

I turned toward the stage again. She was back up there, clapping out the beat. Her cheeks were pink, and the silver studs around her collar twinkled. Except for Gracie and me, everyone in the audience seemed to be clapping along with her.

Ms. Alverson—that was Lexanne's mom—she was always telling me, "Go on and make friends. She's just about your age." But I only ever saw Miranda at the show. The Reyes family did not leave their motor home much. They did not stop for the cookouts we had at state parks and public beaches to break up long drives between towns. They didn't even come out to the Food Pavilion after closing two nights ago when we all sang "Happy Birthday" to Maria Bean and she blew out eight candles on the special seven-layer strawberry-and-whipped-cream funnel cake Mrs. Perez made her.

Onstage, Miranda took off her hat, flicked it up with her fingertips, and caught it on her head.

More whistles. More cheers.

Even if I had gotten to know her, that wasn't the same as making friends. I didn't care what Ms. Alverson said, Miranda did not look like the kind of girl who would want to be friends with me. She was *main-stage material*, after all. She had silver roses stitched onto the sides of her gleaming white cowboy boots. I had silver duct tape holding my sandal together after one of the pygmy goats chewed through the ankle strap.

"All right, all right," Mr. Barsetti said finally. "Miranda y los Reyes can open the main-stage show tonight. Just three songs, Reyes. We'll see if she has what it takes."

"Oh, you'll see," Mr. Reyes said. "You'll see she's outgrown this side stage, and you'd better start treating us like a main attraction before we find someone else who will. And that means a main-attraction paycheck. The kids'll need new costumes, new equipment—"

Mr. Barsetti coughed. *Good luck, Mr. Reyes*, I thought. *You've been here all summer, maybe, but obviously not long enough to know what happens when you ask Mr. Barsetti for a raise.*

I remembered when Mamá and Papá asked for just a little extra money so we could keep on buying premium feed for the silkie chickens. "Well, you know, we're only just squeaking by as it is and, and..." Coughing the whole time like the idea had gotten caught in his lungs or something.

Mr. Reyes tried again. "It's only fair."

Cough. "Fair is fair," Mr. Barsetti said. "But all that rain in July—it was a real blow to attendance, you know. No one saw it coming." *Cough.* "And, of course, there's always the rising cost of gas to keep up with. And insurance. Insurance!" *Cough.* "You would not believe…" His voice trailed off. He cleared his throat. "I'd love to pay you more. Really, I would. But it's just not possible, you understand. Not without cutting someone else."

That was when Papá and Mamá had stopped arguing with him, when Papá put his hand on my shoulder and we turned around and walked back to our trailer.

Not Mr. Reyes.

"So you cut someone else. How much funnel cake do you really need out there? How many roller-skating clowns?"

First of all, there was only one Cordelia Cornflower, and you could not get rid of her. Barsetti would never go for it.

"Or why not cut the petting zoo? I can't believe those things aren't against the law, anyway. Can't be good for the animals. Can't be *clean*."

I nearly spit out a mouthful of half-chewed kettle corn. I wished I could take back Gracie's balloon and smack Mr. Reyes on the forehead with it. Or at least that I was brave enough to turn around and tell him myself how well we took care of our animals. How we were a family, all of us at Barsetti & Son. We were supposed to look out for one another. Mr. Barsetti knew it, though. He would say so for me.

Except he didn't.

Instead, he made that growly noise again. "I don't know about against the law," he said. "But I do know Maldonado isn't bringing in crowds the way he used to. Maybe it's time to make some changes." He coughed one more time. "I'm putting your kids on the big stage tonight, Reyes. Let's see how they do. Then we'll talk."

I stood right up. I put my head right down, and sweat-sticky curls tumbled into my eyes. Lucky for me I didn't let Mamá trim my bangs when she tried to three weeks ago, since I wouldn't have wanted everyone at the Family Side Stage to see me so red-faced and almost about to cry. Then, holding on to my bag of kettle corn like it was the only thing keeping me from flying away, I ran right out of there.

Miranda

(1:15 P.M.)

Well, it wasn't like no one had ever left in the middle of a show before. "You can't take it personally," I mumbled, shrugging off my vest and passing it to Ronnie.

I set my cowboy hat on the shelf, trading it for my Bakersfield Outlaws ball cap. I was seven the first time I sang the national anthem at their stadium. We hadn't missed the home opener in the four years since.

Next year, though? Well, I had no idea where we'd be next year. Either back home or out on the road someplace. It all depended on how well we did this summer. Lately it seemed like *everything*, our whole lives, depended on how well we did this summer. How well *I* did. And there were only a few weeks of summer left.

I shook my head as if I could shake all the worry out, and tried not to think about it. I pulled off my boots and laced up my old Keds.

"Take what personally?"

"Nothing." I ducked as Junior tossed his vest over my head. It landed right on top of mine in Ronnie's arms.

Cold, hard fact: Audiences did not always give us their full and complete attention when we performed. Sometimes they ate in the middle of our shows.

Okay, it wasn't just sometimes, it was more like *always*. Corn dogs. Cotton candy. Whatever. Once, in Salinas, this lady and her kids sat right up near the stage, where people liked to dance, you know? Well, then she opened her purse and pulled out a blanket and—I'm not even kidding—spread out a picnic with little plates and cups and everything. Well, I couldn't help it. I wasn't like Ronnie. Ronnie could've kept on smiling if that lady had brought a whole banquet to the show instead of just a picnic. Mom always said Ronnie had poise. But not me.

"You know, looking at all your food is making me kinda hungry. So, unless you plan to share, could you save it till after the show?" Everyone laughed. Even the lady with the picnic.

Dad didn't think it was very funny, though. "Mija, you

need to focus," he had told me later. "You're a *performer*. You can't let the distractions get to you. Ignore them."

But it was hard to focus when people made phone calls during our shows, not to mention when they changed their babies' diapers. And it was almost impossible to ignore it when someone walked out, let alone when someone *ran*.

"Hey, Ronnie?"

"Hey, what?" My sister had taken the vests to the back of the motor home where Mom and Dad slept, to hang them.

"Did you see that girl? The one who ran out of the show? Curly hair? Green-and-white shirt? It was in the middle of 'Esta Rosa Roja'?"

The closet door closed with a soft thud, and Ronnie came back out to the middle of the motor home. Wicked Wanda's belly, I liked to think, since that was where the kitchen was.

Ronnie tapped her knuckles against her forehead like she was really thinking hard about it. "Mmm...Nope. Didn't notice anyone. All I noticed during 'Esta Rosa Roja' was Junior playing too fast again."

"Not my fault if you can't keep up." He was slurping Spaghetti-Os straight out of the can.

"Gross," Ronnie said. "Use a spoon at least." She reached around me, into the drawer under the sink. "Here."

It probably wasn't such a big deal. I wouldn't have even noticed her if she hadn't run right by—practically right *into*— Dad and Mr. Barsetti.

14

Dad was trying, yet again, to talk Mr. Barsetti into paying us more. If it didn't work, I had heard Mom whisper to Dad a few nights earlier, we would just have to accept that it was time to go home. Cold, hard fact.

I slid into the L-shaped booth next to Junior. You wouldn't believe it to see it, but the booth and table pulled out into a bed with enough room for Ronnie and me to share. Junior's bunk was right over the steering wheel.

He handed me the can, and I scooped up a big bite of Spaghetti-Os.

"Ooh, with hot dog!" I thought we were out of those. I shoveled another bite into my mouth before Junior grabbed the can back.

"You guys!" Ronnie screeched. "So gross. *So* gross. We still have a microwave. We still have *bowls.*"

She pulled a box of cereal off the shelf and took it to the driver's seat.

So someone ran out of our show. No big deal. Just forget it.

Except it was kind of like a mosquito bite. The more I tried to ignore it, the worse it itched. "But why would she run out right in the middle of a song? It's a good song. Everyone loves the 'Rosa Roja' song."

At least I thought they did. By the end, there was always a bunch of people singing along. There was always a moment when I couldn't tell my voice from their voices anymore, or even from Ronnie's accordion or Junior's guitar. It was just one big, bright sound that rocketed up into the sky like fireworks, leaving a trail of sparkles behind.

But maybe I was wrong. Maybe the whole act was getting boring. Maybe that girl was just the beginning, and soon whole rows of people would leave right in the middle of a song. Or worse, stop showing up to begin with.

It had all been for me, and it would've all been for nothing.

Junior swallowed. He scraped the last drops of tomato sauce from the bottom of the can.

"Do you think maybe she just couldn't stand listening to your Spanish anymore, Miss *Ro-zah Ro-hah*?"

I socked him on the shoulder. "*Stop.* It's not that bad."

"Do you even know what you're singing about?"

Not every word, not exactly. But I was pretty sure I understood the main ideas. "Love," I said.

"Yeah, and?"

"And a rose. A red one. Whatever."

The only reason Ronnie and Junior could speak Spanish was because Tía Elena, who spoke *only* Spanish, used to babysit them when they were little. But not me. And it wasn't like I wasn't *trying* to learn. As Wicked Wanda rumbled over the highway from fair to fair, I listened to *You Can Speak Spanish! The Complete Audio Course.* Dad had found it at a gas station in Wilton.

Hola. ¿Cómo está?
Hello. How are you?

Bien, gracias. ¿Y usted?

Well, thank you. And you?

Even Dad said I was getting better. Junior just liked to give me a hard time.

Ronnie swiveled around to face us, cereal box still on her lap. "Randy, let it go. You can't make everyone like you. So some girl left in the middle of the show. Who cares? She was probably late meeting up with her mom or something. If I were you, I'd be more worried about that stunt you pulled, jumping off the stage."

"*Stunt?* Come on, the crowd loved it." They did too. That, at least, I was sure about. When I had seen everyone dancing down there, I just sorta knew I should dance with them. So I jumped. Didn't even have to think about it.

Ronnie said "*Mmmm*" and swiveled away.

"Junior, tell her. It was practically the best part of the whole show, everyone screaming, all surprised and excited like the piñata just broke."

Junior straightened up and threw back his shoulders. "We did not rehearse jumping off the stage," he said, scrunching up his nose and bunching up his eyebrows and sounding almost exactly like Dad. "Stick with what we rehearse!"

"We rehearse for a reason!" I boomed, doing my own impersonation.

"You better be quiet," Ronnie warned in her bossy-as-usual voice. She threw a handful of Froot Loops at us. Junior caught one in his mouth.

Just then, there was a tap on the kitchen window. We all froze.

"Verónica? Junior? Miranda? Are you in there? Can one of you get the door?"

We exhaled. Only Mom.

Ronnie got up to let her in while Junior and I swept cereal crumbs off the table. We finished just as Mom dropped an armful of fresh-from-the-laundromat socks and T-shirts on top of it.

She cracked her neck, first to the right, then to the left. "Randy, mija, fold those while I sit down for a minute?"

The laundry was already folded, but before we could put it away, we had to fold it all over again. There was only one drawer for each of us inside Wicked Wanda, and the clothes didn't fit unless they were *extra* flat.

"You didn't walk, did you, Ma?" Junior asked.

She sank into the passenger seat and loosened her shoelaces. "No, no, mijo. One of the carnival ladies gave me a ride. It's just so hot out there, and the laundromat didn't have air-conditioning." She looked around. "Is your father here? How did things go with Barsetti?"

"Don't know," Ronnie said. "He hasn't come back yet."

Mom frowned. "Well, we'll find out when we find out. You're finished for the weekend anyway."

And maybe forever. She didn't have to say it out loud.

She unzipped her purse and took out three rolls of quarters.

I knew from all the times I went with her to the laundromat that each one held forty coins. Ten dollars. "And I think you should celebrate," she said, holding them out to us.

We all froze again.

"Go on, take them. My arm's getting tired."

Junior and Ronnie looked at me. It didn't matter that I was the youngest, it was always up to me to say the things that no one else wanted to say. So I cleared my throat and touched Mom's elbow. "Mom, that is the laundry money," I said. Slowly, like maybe Mom had forgotten.

It was only when she laughed like she laughed right then that I could see myself in Mom's face. A gap between her two front teeth, and eyes that crinkled at the corners. People usually said we looked just like Dad with our round cheeks and thick black eyebrows.

"Thank you, mija. Yes, I know it's the laundry money," she said. "I'm the one who goes out searching for a laundromat every weekend, remember?"

"So, then, don't you need it for next week?" Junior asked, leaning on the edge of the table.

Mom stared at the rolls of quarters, then looked back up at us.

"Depending on what Mr. Barsetti tells your father today, next week we'll either have more quarters, or..."

Or?

"Or," Mom continued, "we won't. So help Miranda finish

19

the folding, then take the money and go have fun. You've been to how many carnivals this summer? And haven't had a chance to enjoy even one of them. Ándale. Go."

She meant, "Go before Dad gets back and says it's time to rehearse again." We all knew it.

Junior pushed himself off the table and took the quarters from Mom. He lobbed one roll to Ronnie and one to me, then tossed his own in the air and caught it. "I think I'll try a frozen lemonade."

"You'll try a frozen lemonade," I said, coiling a pair of white socks. "Or you'll try to get Lexanne to talk to you?" Lexanne and her mom had a little red car. They gave Ronnie and me rides to the grocery store sometimes when Mom didn't feel like taking Wanda out. Junior was always trying to find some excuse to tag along, but mostly Dad made him stay behind to polish the boots.

Junior pulled the brim of my hat down over my eyes. "See you, Ro-zah."

But he stopped when he got to the door. "Dad!"

Wanda shook as Dad stomped on the mat to shake the dust off his shoes. He flung his hat on top of the laundry pile and squeezed Junior's shoulders. "Heading out to rehearse, *mijo*? Good. Because you're still racing through the chorus."

He turned to my sister. "Verónica? You go out and help him count. And, mijo, remember, you are the backbone. Keep it strong and steady: *Bom, bom, bom, bom.*" He clapped with every beat.

Then he stopped and put his hands on his hips. "Where's Miranda?"

I lifted my head above the laundry pile.

"Ah. Mija, make yourself some tea. But first, go wash off your face. You been hanging around the clown car?"

Not again. "Dad, it's a carnival, not a circus. There's no clown car. And anyway, it's just makeup. Not even that much."

"Off. You're, what, ten?"

"Eleven." Not that it mattered. Not that he'd *ever* stop telling me what to do or what to wear or who to be.

I slid out of the booth and into the bathroom, which was smaller than the coat closet back at our old house. So small that if I stretched my arms out I could touch the door with one hand and the back wall with the other. Some of the people who traveled with Barsetti & Son—like Lexanne and her mom—got to stay in motels every weekend. Some of the motels even had swimming pools, Lexanne told me. Must've been nice to dive into a pool after a long, sweaty day at the fair, I couldn't help thinking. Must've been nice to stay in a room it took more than three steps to walk across.

Still, I reminded myself, a lot of the other carnival workers slept in tents and trailers. She might have been small, but I had a feeling Wicked Wanda was a lot more comfortable than a tent pitched on a gravel parking lot.

"And don't think we aren't going to discuss you jumping off the stage this afternoon," Dad called after me. "We did not rehearse jumping off the stage. Stick with what we rehearse."

I stuck the quarters in my pocket. We hadn't gotten out fast enough, and just like always, fun would have to wait. I turned on the faucet and scrubbed away Mom's red lipstick and Ronnie's inky mascara with Dad's bar of clean, white soap. It even *smelled* serious.

The bathroom door barely muffled the sounds outside. Cupboard doors opened and shut as Dad rummaged for the bag of chicharrones that Mom kept hiding, and then for the old pocket notebook where he scribbled out our set lists. I didn't know why he even bothered. We always played the same songs in exactly the same order.

But if there was one thing Dad loved, it was a plan. He treated plans like secret recipes. No substitutions, no skipping steps. He was flipping through the notebook when I stepped out of the bathroom, water dripping off my chin.

We all watched him, Mom, Ronnie, Junior, and me.

He looked up.

"What's everyone staring at? Why aren't you rehearsing?"

Mom stood. Her lips were thin and straight. No more gappy smile. "Barsetti, Lalo. What did he say?"

Dad scratched his head. He whistled through his teeth. "What he always says."

Mom's chin dropped.

I gnawed on my thumbnail, stopped myself, and laced my fingers behind my back.

"Well," Mom said. "Well."

Dad didn't say anything. His face was still and stony—until finally, his mouth twitched. Only a little, but enough for me to know he was hiding something. Something good.

I stepped forward, pushing Junior aside, and grabbed Dad's arm.

"What?" I asked, shaking him. "Tell us."

Dad looked down at me, at all of us. Made sure the spotlight was shining right on him. Like the dream he'd had since he was my age had finally come true, and *he* was lead singer of los Reyes. Then his mouth twitched itself into a grin.

"He said Miranda y los Reyes is playing the main stage tonight!"

Ronnie jumped and threw her arms around Dad's waist, nearly knocking him over. He laughed as he stumbled backward, just catching himself before they both fell. Junior pulled my hat off and ruffled my hair. "You did it, sis."

I kept my hands pressed over my mouth. Otherwise, they would have heard me screaming all the way back at the laundromat.

Only three songs, Dad explained. We were *only* the opening act.

Well, maybe it was only three songs, but it was also the

only reason we were there: to play on a real stage—even bigger than the side stage—not just at wedding receptions and quinceañeras, or in the dim corners of taquerías. Ronnie grabbed me and Junior and pulled us into her hug.

Only Mom was missing.

"Lalo?"

We broke apart and looked at her.

"But what about the money? Is he going to pay?"

Dad took her by the hands and drew her toward him. Then he dipped her over his arm like it was the end of a tango. "He will when he sees them."

He lifted Mom to her feet and pointed to the rest of us, one by one.

"So we have to be perfect tonight," he said. "Really connect."

Connect.

Exactly.

That was the problem. I wasn't connecting. I couldn't, not really, not when I didn't understand half the words. But I knew what to do.

"I have the perfect song."

"I'm still thinking about that," Dad said, remembering his notebook. "For now, rehearse the usual set." He started flipping pages again.

"No, something else. Wait, it's right here." In my drawer, under my clothes, I found the composition book Ms. McDaniel had given me on my last day in her class that spring. It was a week before fifth grade was supposed to end, and she had tried to persuade my parents to let me stay and finish the year. But the carnival wouldn't wait, so neither could we.

When I had closed my eyes, I could see a road map with little yellow stars next to all the new cities we would visit. I could hear the cheers of audiences bigger than any we had ever played for. There were one hundred eighty-five seats at the Family Side Stage. One hundred eighty-five! I couldn't keep my hands still. It was like I was filled with soda fizz after someone had just shaken the bottle.

And yet, thinking about everything we would miss when we were gone, about all our friends moving on without us, had felt a little like being left behind. Even though we were the ones going away. It was the same hollow-stomach feeling I had one Monday morning, a year or so before we left, when I found out all the other girls in our class had been to Lisa Li's house for a sleepover that weekend. I wasn't invited.

"I didn't think you could come," Lisa had explained. "You're always busy singing on the weekends." She was right, but that didn't make it feel any better.

I tried to explain it all to Ms. McDaniel, and that was when she gave me the composition book. She said it was a journal for writing down everything I saw and thought and felt while we were on the road.

So far, there wasn't anything in the notebook except for just the one song. Between rehearsals and Spanish lessons and Dad's lectures on discipline, sacrifice, and stage presence, there wasn't time for much else.

But it was all right. One song was all we needed.

"What's this?" Dad asked.

"It's nothing," Ronnie said before I could answer.

Junior tried to snatch the book out of my fingers. "Randy, no. We were just having fun. He's not going to go for it."

But it wasn't nothing. "It's a new song," I said. "Well, not exactly a new song. It's an old song. But a new version. Our own version. We wrote it, Junior and Ronnie and me. And it's perfect for tonight."

It really was.

See, we always ended our show with this song called "El Rey." Because our last name was Reyes, I guess, and because it was Dad's favorite. It was about this guy who, even though he didn't have any money or anyone to love him, still felt like a king. The king of his own life.

To help me work on my Spanish, Ronnie translated it with me, line by line. That's how I got the idea to translate it again. Into my own words, words that meant something to me. Words about hoping so hard your heart hurts. Junior sped it up a little and we practiced every now and then, when Dad wasn't around.

"Come on, you guys. Play with me."

Ronnie looked at the floor. Junior rubbed the back of his neck.

"Miranda, we don't have time for—" Dad started to say.

"Go ahead," Mom interrupted. "I want to hear it."

Junior and Ronnie looked at each other.

"Come *on*," I said again.

Ronnie started humming, so quietly I could barely hear her. Junior took a spoon from the sink and drummed it against the countertop. I closed my eyes and sang.

We got through a verse before Ronnie went quiet and Junior stopped tapping. "That's about it," he said, his voice like a candle flame that flickered and flickered until it was finally out. "The rest of it is...just...sort of...like that."

Mom clapped.

"Lalo," she said when Dad did not.

He sucked a big breath in through his teeth and blew it out through his nose. "It's nice, Miranda. You kids did a nice job. But this is not main-stage material. Not tonight. You'll sing the song the right way." He pressed his palms together. "Verónica and Junior? Go. Practice. Now." He shooed them off. "Miranda, make some tea. And enough talking. You need to rest your voice."

He opened the cupboard and took out a coffee mug and the box of Lipton.

"The *right* way?"

Dad paused, staring a few seconds into the still-open cupboard before answering me.

"Yes, Miranda, the way I taught you." He closed the cupboard. *Bam.* Like he was closing the discussion too.

But I couldn't let him. We had worked on that song most of the summer. I was saving it for just the right time, and this was it. I knew it was. This would work.

"We already sang it that way," I said. "We always sing it that way. *Your* way. Why can't we sing it *my* way for once? This is *my* chance, after all."

Ronnie and Junior crept backward, but they couldn't escape.

And even though I knew I should let it go, I couldn't seem to stop myself. "We have to dress your way, play your way. Maybe you should just sing it yourself."

"Enough!" Dad slapped his hands against the counter, so hard I felt the sting in my own fingers. "After everything we've given up, after how far we've come, after everything we've planned..."

Mom stepped between us. "Miranda, go outside. Take a walk."

"She needs to prepare," Dad said, his voice lower again. So low it was almost a whisper.

"She needs a walk." Mom was practically pushing me out the door.

Flor

(1:10 P.M.)

With one hand still holding tight to the kettle corn bag and the other balled into an angry fist, fingernails digging into my palms, I marched through the midway and back to the petting zoo. I had to force my legs not to run. I did not want to call attention to myself, not with my cheeks still so hot. But I couldn't help feeling like, if I didn't get back there quickly, Rancho Maldonado would be shut down and boarded up before I could save it. Because the thing of it was, I had noticed our lines getting shorter, the crowds getting thinner all summer. What I hadn't realized was that Mr. Barsetti had noticed too.

Why not cut the petting zoo? Just thinking about it made

my eyes sting. And I could not believe I had wasted every lunch hour since Bakersfield watching Monstrous Miranda and the Rotten Reyes family getting ready to bump us off the carnival lineup.

It did not matter that she didn't mean to, or that she probably didn't know the petting zoo even existed. Depending on how she sang tonight—and since I *had* wasted every lunch hour watching her, I knew exactly how she'd sing—Miranda could be the final straw, the reason Rancho Maldonado closed for good. And that would make one more reason for Mamá to take me home and send me back to regular school. I sped up. Normally it took around ten minutes to walk halfway across the fairgrounds, from Rancho Maldonado to the side stage. That afternoon, I got there in five.

"Slow down. Where's the fire? You too busy to even say hello anymore?"

I had just walked past the frozen lemonade stand. It was screaming yellow and shaped like an enormous lemon. Not the sort of thing you just walked past, unless of course, you happened to walk past it almost every single day. Ms. Alverson was leaning out the window.

"Sorry, I was just trying to get to the zoo. I'm running a little late. Told Papá I'd be right back."

"The zoo's not going anywhere," she said. "Hold up a minute."

I hoped it wasn't going anywhere. But after what I'd heard

at the side stage, I couldn't be sure. Ms. Alverson helped the next customers in line. It was a dad and two kids, and each of them carried one of those handheld water-spritzing fans you could buy at a carnival concession stand for eight or ten dollars—or, like, two bucks anywhere else. But they must have thought it was worth the price. When you're sweaty, you're sweaty, I guess.

The kids were already holding corn dogs and barbecue turkey drumsticks bigger than their arms. I didn't know how they were going to juggle the lemonades too, but somehow, they managed, sort of hugging the frosty cups against their sides as they shambled toward a picnic table.

After Ms. Alverson called out after them to have a nice day, she told Lexanne to come and watch the stand for a couple of minutes. Lexanne had been stretched out on a beach towel, studying the *Diseases of the Teeth and Gums* book we all pitched in to buy her last May when she earned her GED. She was leaving for college in three weeks and wanted to become a dentist someday. Ms. Alverson tossed her an apron, then met me outside, carrying two large frozen lemonades.

She wiped her forehead on her sleeve. "What I need is one of those mini water fans everyone's walking around with. Here. Take these."

Two weeks earlier, right after the Dry Bean Festival in Tracy, Mamá had said good-bye and taken the bus over to Stockton. My Tía Patty had a house there and found her a

31

job. A good one at a doctor's office. But before she left, Mamá made Ms. Alverson promise to look out for Papá and me.

And since then, Ms. Alverson didn't seem to think she was keeping her word unless she was filling us up with frozen lemonade.

"You look like you could use something cool to drink, all red in the face like that. And goodness knows, your father hasn't taken a break all morning. He takes better care of those animals than he does himself."

She was right about that.

We didn't always have the petting zoo, but we'd had animals since forever. We used to live on a little farm out in the country, with cherry trees and chickens and goats and rabbits. The Ranch, we called it. Papá invited my kindergarten class out for a visit once, to see the animals and feed them. Everyone had such a good time that when the first-grade teachers heard about it, they asked to bring their classes too. After a while, pretty much every school in the city was calling to schedule a field trip. Papá didn't mind, though. He loved telling kids about how one pound of sheep's wool can make ten *miles* of yarn. Or how chickens can fly, just not very far and not very high.

I didn't mind either. On farm days, no one ever said a word about my jacket with sleeves that were too short, or about the chicken feathers stuck to my backpack. Everyone looked at Papá like he was in charge and he had all the answers.

Then, one weekend, a man in a suit and cowboy hat showed

up. He'd heard about the Ranch from his niece, he said, and he wondered, had Papá ever considered taking the animals out on the road?

"You'd be surprised how many kids out there don't know where eggs come from, never milked a cow before."

"We don't have a cow," Papá said.

"My point is," the man persisted, "a wholesome, back-to-basics act like this would be a big hit on the carnival circuit. We'd pay you, of course. Why don't you come along with us for the summer, see how it goes?"

Papá said thanks but no. He wasn't sure how the animals—not to mention Mamá and me—would take to it, all that traveling. The Ranch was staying put.

So the man said good-bye. He left a business card, just in case Papá ever changed his mind: Mr. Albert Barsetti, Barsetti & Son All-American Extravaganzas. There was a picture of a Ferris wheel on the back side.

But it turned out the Ranch wasn't staying put after all. See, the land wasn't actually ours, we just rented it. And about a year after Mr. Barsetti came to visit, the owner told us he needed the property back. He paid us for the cherry orchard, but the animals had to go. Only, without the barn and without a pasture, we weren't sure where.

"We could sell them," Mamá said one night at dinner, pushing green beans around her plate with the edge of a spoon. "We might have to."

But I wasn't ready, and neither was Papá. He dug that business card out of his wallet and called up Mr. Barsetti. We spent some of our savings, plus the cherry tree money, on a trailer for the animals and an RV for us, and a month later, Rancho Maldonado Petting Zoo made its debut at the Calaveras County Fair.

We only planned to stay with the carnival for the summer, just long enough to find a new house on another big piece of land. But it turned out things weren't so bad on the circuit. We got to see a new city every weekend, the animals seemed to like all the attention, and there were even other kids around. Nine of us altogether. So when summer ended, instead of starting fourth grade, I started road-schooling with Mikey and Maria Bean. Mikey was my age, and Maria was three years younger. Their dad worked rides and games, and their mom set up a little classroom next to Mr. Barsetti's office where we all went for lessons Thursday through Monday, while the rest of the adults were working. Tuesday and Wednesday were usually traveling days, but Mrs. Bean always made sure we had a reading assignment to work on. We got summers off, just like we would have if we didn't live on the road.

"Looks like your dad has a little crowd over there," Ms. Alverson said, pointing to the zoo. Before turning around, I shut my eyes and wished that when I opened them, Rancho Maldonado would be packed. I wished for a long line of people, all waiting to pet the goats or feed the sheep. There were lines everywhere else, after all. Lines to buy sausage and peppers, lines to speed down a slide on a burlap sack, lines to throw dull darts at a wall of balloons that almost never popped.

I looked.

When Ms. Alverson said "little," she must have meant small. As in short. Besides Maria—who didn't count because she was always hanging around and wasn't a paying customer, anyway—the only "crowd" at Rancho Maldonado was twin toddlers and their grinning parents. Papá watched the boys waddle through the wood shavings, arms stretched out in front of them like drooly zombies, while their parents stood back and took pictures. Mikey told me that at some carnivals they charged for pictures with the animals, and he thought we could build a photo booth and start a business, him and me. We wouldn't have to charge too much—even a little bit more money would help. Papá would never agree to it, though.

"Your papá has a generous heart," Mamá said once as we watched him give our old sleeping bag away to one of the newer workers who was sleeping in a tent with just a thin blanket. She had sounded a little sad when she said it, though, and I didn't understand why, since I always thought generous was a good thing to be.

But since she'd left, I was beginning to see how, when it came to running a business, Papá's generous heart sometimes got in the way of his head.

"San Joaquin County next week," Ms. Alverson said, interrupting my thoughts.

"Yeah."

"Excited to see your mom?"

I sighed.

Mamá had wanted to take me with her. She said it was time for me to live in the real world again, to go back to school. To start sixth grade.

But Papá was going to stay with the carnival—Tía Patty might have found Mamá a job, but she had not found a new home for the animals—and I didn't want to leave either.

"You can stay for the summer," Mamá had compromised.

"Forever."

"We'll see."

I thought if I could convince them Papá needed my help running the zoo, she might change her mind. But there was no way Mamá would let me stay if she knew Rancho Maldonado was in danger of closing.

I watched Papá shake hands with the toddlers' parents. Then he patted each boy's strawberry-blond head.

"How's she getting along with your aunt?"

"Huh?" I had not been paying attention.

"Your mom," Ms. Alverson said. "How's she doing? She must miss you two."

"Oh, she's fine, I guess." She was probably fine, but I had only talked to her twice since she left. She usually called on her lunch break, which just happened to be at the same time as my daily trip to the Family Side Stage. All she wanted to talk about was school and how much I would love going back. But every time she mentioned it, all I could think about was sitting alone in that crowded cafeteria, or listening to giggly whispers fly behind me in class, never being sure what they were saying exactly, but knowing it was about me just the same.

Inside the animal pen, Papá handed each of the twin boys a brown paper bag full of oats and seeds.

For free.

I ground my teeth. It was like he didn't even care whether Rancho Maldonado survived. Like no one ever told him we were supposed to be running a business. Mamá had tried, but with her gone, it was all up to me.

"Sorry, Ms. Alverson, I have to go. Thanks for the lemonade."

Each bag of animal feed cost one dollar. Said so right on the sign. People loved letting the animals eat out of their hands, kids especially. It was one of the only reasons they came at all. And Papá was just *giving* it away.

I jogged up to the wood-and-wire fencing that surrounded the zoo and forced the words out: "That'll be two dollars." My voice sounded small and shaky. No one even heard me. So I cleared my throat and tried again. "The feed costs a dollar a bag. So that's two dollars... please."

"Oh!" The mom looked up, all startled and embarrassed,

and reached into her pocket. Her cheeks were as pink as mine felt. "Of course, just let me…"

Papá stared at me openmouthed like I had just told her she needed to buy the rooster a tennis racket or something.

"No, no," he said, touching the woman on the elbow. "It's on me. I insist. You just enjoy this time with your boys. It goes by so fast."

"But, *Papá*."

"Flor, if we can't afford a little kindness, it isn't worth staying in business."

It was only two dollars. But two dollars is two dollars, you know? And sure, Ms. Alverson had just given us free lemonade. But that was different. She was looking out for us, and so was I—only, Papá was making it so difficult.

"Fine. Enjoy." I wrenched my mouth into a smile and set the lemonades on the ticket counter. "Maria, you can have mine."

"Thanks!" she chirped.

"And from now on," I whispered into her ear, "*you're* in charge of selling the oats." Then I went around back to the shed behind the petting zoo. It was where we stacked the feed and hay, and where we took the animals to rest when they needed a break from people. It was also where we kept Betabel.

Her name meant sugar beet, after the harvest where Mamá and Papá first met. But she wasn't very sweet.

"Where are you, Betabel? Come out." She did not come.

"Betabel? Come on, pretty piggy." Nothing. Not a sound. I shook the bag of kettle corn. "I have treats."

That did it. Betabel snuffled and swaggered out from a shady corner of the shed. I shook a handful of popcorn into my hand and held it out for her to sniff.

She wagged her tail and lifted her snout in the air. Then I closed my fist and took my hand away. "Not so fast."

We had gotten Betabel a year before at the county fair in Marin. This guy walked into the petting zoo with her and took Papá aside. He told us he hadn't known she'd grow so big, that he couldn't keep her in his apartment anymore, and could we take her? Then he offered us a bunch of money.

Papá said to put the money away and of course we could help. Mamá rubbed her temples and bit her lip.

"But Mario. A pig?"

He put his hands on his hips and smiled to himself. "The kids will like to play with a pig, ¿que no?"

"¡Que sí!" I answered for him, dropping to my knees to scratch behind the pig's ears. "They will *love* it."

But it turned out Betabel didn't want to have anything to do with kids. Or anyone else, really, except for Papá and me.

Fortunately, Papá had found a potbellied pig farm near Dinuba, and the owner was supposed to come out and take a look at her, to see if he could help us.

For now, she was strictly backstage only.

But at least you always knew where you stood with Betabel.

You never had to worry she was only pretending to like you, that she'd be nice to you one minute and bite you when your back was turned. You could respect a pig like that.

And, anyway, I had a feeling Betabel had untapped potential.

See, back in Turlock, in between fairs, Papá and I went to check out another carnival, one run by Sierra Vista Amusements, Barsetti's only real rival. Sierra Vista had this skateboarding pug named Puccini, and people would stand in line for an hour to see him. Three times a day. In 102-degree heat. And when the show was over, they stood in line all over again to buy T-shirts and sun visors and water bottles and key chains, all with a picture of Puccini on them.

It gave me an idea. Betabel might not have been sweet, but she was smart. Smarter than some dog, anyway. I had been trying to train her to ride a skateboard ever since then, and she was finally making progress.

"It's now or never," I told her. "It's all up to us. Pig versus pop star."

I rolled the skateboard out of the shed. Mikey had given it to me after he got a new one at the flea market. The deck was pretty banged up, and one of the wheels was loose, but that didn't matter, not for practice. I was saving up the nickels and dimes I found near the trash bins—people were always throwing away their loose change by accident—to buy something nicer for when Betabel was ready for an audience.

The first step was to get her comfortable standing on the board. I dropped a few pieces of kettle corn on it. She waddled over, ate them, and stepped off when she was finished. "Good girl," I told her. "You got this."

I reached into the bag and scattered a little more popcorn on the board. Only this time, when she stepped on and started chewing, I added another handful. Then, before she was finished, I gently pushed the skateboard forward a few inches. And then a few inches more. It bobbled over the hard-packed dirt.

Betabel lifted her head and grunted.

"All right, all right, I'm sorry." I gave her some more kettle corn. "Here you go. See? It's not so bad. You can do this. You were *born* for this."

But just as I was getting ready to give the skateboard another push, a shriek rang out from the petting zoo. Betabel hopped off the skateboard and scuttled back inside the shed. I sprang off the ground, dropped the bag of kettle corn on the counter, and rushed over. It could have been a chicken pecking someone's ankle. Or worse, one of the goats mistaking some kid's finger for a French fry. It had happened before, and it was never good. Angry customers were almost worse than no customers at all.

I scrambled around to the animal pen, and when I saw what the fuss was about, I threw my head back and groaned. The Fairest of the Fair, all of them in white summer dresses and high-heeled sandals, turquoise sashes draped over their chests. The one in the middle—this was Dinuba, I remembered, so she must have been the Cantaloupe Queen—wore a glittery crown.

Just like every fair had a local band, each one had a pageant. The Peach Blossom Princesses or the Dairy Debutantes. Whoever they were, whatever town they were from, they always stopped by Rancho Maldonado for a portrait with the animals.

"One of them gave Chivo a cookie," Maria whispered, then sucked the last droplets of frozen lemonade through her straw. "And then he licked her finger trying to get the crumbs too. That's how come she screamed."

"Didn't she see the sign?" I had made it myself: PLEASE DON'T FEED THE ANIMALS. UNLESS IT'S ANIMAL FEED—$1 A BAG.

"I tried to tell her."

Maria and I stood in the back of the pen and watched as Papá offered the girl a wad of paper towels and some hand sanitizer, while the photographer tried to guide the rest of the Cantaloupe Court into two straight lines. "All right, ladies, all right. Just a few more shots. Can one of you hold the rabbit? Scoot in a little closer, *aaaaand* perfect."

Barsetti was there, standing next to the photographer with his hands behind his back. Only he wasn't watching the Cantaloupe Court, he was studying the zoo. I tried to see it the way he must have. Four goats, five chickens, three bunnies, and a sheep, munching on hay and burrowing in the wood shavings. Wire fencing wrapped around skinny wood posts. Nearly empty.

But there was so much more he couldn't see. Like how Papá had been teaching Maria how to trim the sheep's hooves because she wanted to be a veterinarian when she grew up. Or how, that Thursday before the fair opened, when we were setting up, he traded spots with Ms. Alverson so Lexanne would have some shade while she studied. Maybe we would have had a bigger crowd if we hadn't set the zoo up in the sun.

"Hey, isn't that Libby? It is! Libby, you're back!" Maria started hopping and waving her arms.

I looked closer. It was hard to tell at first because her hair was shorter now, but Maria was right. Liberty Chavez. Her dad was a mechanic and they used to travel with the carnival until someone offered him a better job—in Dinuba. They'd left us after last year's fair. Mr. Barsetti had been furious.

Libby looked over her shoulder and fluttered her fingers at Maria and me, but she didn't say hello. She just turned right back around and smiled at the camera.

Maria's shoulders dropped, and she wrinkled her nose. "Oh," she said. "I guess she didn't hear me."

I nodded and squeezed Maria's shoulder. Libby had heard. But with new friends like that, why would she ever want to admit she had been one of us? That was the way it was outside the carnival. Maria didn't know because she had never lived anyplace else. She was practically born on the midway.

The photographer slung her camera strap over her neck. "I think I've got what I need here. What's next?"

"Cantaloupe milk shakes," Barsetti said. "And then deep-fried cantaloupe on a stick." He waved at Papá and they all left, the princesses holding up their dresses and tiptoeing over the hay.

Maria tossed the empty lemonade cup into a trash basket. "Well, they're gone. I better go bring out some fresh water."

Maria changed out the animals' water at least once an hour, way more often than we needed to. But Papá had said, "Déjala," so I left her alone and went searching for Chivo, to make sure he was all right after all the commotion.

He was fine, of course. Eating out of some girl's hand as she babbled away to him in the strangest-sounding Spanish I had ever heard.

Miranda

(2 P.M.)

The goat was tiny and black and so much easier to talk to than my dad. He had a white tail and a diamond-shaped patch of white hair right between his eyes. The goat, I mean. Not Dad.

The goat listened.

The goat was patient.

The goat didn't argue.

"I mean, *I'm* the one standing up there and singing in front of everyone. All I was asking was just to *try* something different. *I* have ideas too. ¿Me entiendes? You understand?"

I had a feeling he did. I scratched his nose.

The petting zoo was the only place I could think of to go

when Mom told me to take a walk. It was Lexanne's mom who had first pointed it out to me, one of those times Ronnie and I met her at the lemonade stand for a grocery run. "Have you met Flor yet? She's about your age. Her parents run the petting zoo. You should go visit."

But I never had time to visit. That was because, except for trips to the grocery store or the laundromat, we mostly rehearsed. Or got ready to rehearse. Or talked about how rehearsal had gone.

Well. *Dad* talked about how rehearsal had gone. The rest of us just listened.

Dad had wanted to be a headliner once. Thought he'd rule the whole ranchera scene. Instead, his band broke up right after Ronnie was born, and he became a DJ and wedding singer. Voted number one in Kern County—that's what it said on the side of his van—and that was enough for him.

Until he realized Ronnie and Junior and me could play. Then his dream, like a little seed planted deep in his heart, started growing all over again.

After a while, after I saw how my voice could make people stand up and dance, that little seed started wrapping its roots around *my* heart too. Around all our hearts. We wanted a record deal. We wanted to hear our songs on the radio. We wanted to sign autographs and sell out stadiums.

Except I never stopped wanting all the normal stuff too. Like a pet.

Dad never let us have one, not even a goldfish. We wouldn't have had time to take care of it, he said, and we couldn't take an animal out on the road with us.

"Well, you don't mind being out on the road, do you?" The goat nibbled oats and sunflower seeds out of my hand. The brown paper bag of animal food had cost me a dollar's worth of quarters, and the way he was eating, I had a feeling I was going to have to buy another one pretty soon.

"Tienes hambre," I told him as his rough tongue tickled my palm, searching for more oats. "You're hungry," I said again in English, just like the voice from *You Can Speak Spanish!*

I listened to it so much I had started repeating myself the same way the lady on the recordings did. It really bugged Junior, but I couldn't help it.

I reached into the paper bag, grabbed another handful of oats, and held it out to the goat.

Meh, he bleated happily. *Meh, meh.*

"¿Cómo estás?" I asked him. "How are you?"

"Muy bien, ¿y tu?" I answered in a gravelly, goaty voice. "Very well, and you?"

I felt someone step up behind me. "He doesn't talk back, you know."

"Huh?"

It couldn't have taken more than half a second for me to turn and look up at her. But that was all the time the goat needed to snatch what was left of the oats and devour it, bag and all. Then he came in closer, nosing around my pocket, almost knocking me into a bale of hay.

"Well, I bet if you offered him enough to eat you could get him to talk."

"Yeah, maybe." She laughed, just a little, and pulled the goat off me, but as soon as she let him go, he charged at my pocket again.

"What do you have in there, anyway?"

"Just some quarters," I said, scratching his neck. "That's it," I told the goat. "You ate everything else. Todo."

Meh, the goat said as if he didn't believe me. *Meh*.

"Better watch out," the girl said. "You can't hide anything from Chivo."

"You call your goat . . . Goat?"

She looked at the ground and twisted her toe into the dirt "Why? What else would you call him?"

"I don't know, is that one named Goat too?" I pointed at another little goat, a brown one, napping in the straw.

"No," she said, like it was the most ridiculous thing she'd heard all day. "That's Cricket."

"Hey!" Chivo dove at my pocket again, almost taking a bite out of my denim skirt. "All right, all right. Look, I'll show you. There's nothing in there."

Well, when I reached into my pocket there were quarters but also two Froot Loops. Must've fallen in somehow when Junior and I were throwing them around the Winnebago.

"*This?* This is what you want?"

Meh. Chivo gobbled up the Froot Loops and looked at me, crunching accusingly.

"See? I told you. You cannot hide anything from Chivo." She tapped her fingers against a homemade sign that was stapled to the wall. "And, um, you're not supposed to feed him cereal."

"Well, he didn't exactly ask permission."

The girl brushed her hair out of her eyes.

It was curly and brown.

She wore a green-and-white baseball shirt.

Everything clicked.

I had been pretty far away when I saw her earlier, but I was sure this was the girl from the show. The one who had walked out. Who had *run* out.

"Hey, I've seen you before. Weren't you at the Family Side Stage today?" Maybe I could ask her why she left. Find out what she didn't like, what had gone wrong. "At the lunchtime show? Miranda y los Reyes?"

She had been watching Chivo, but when I asked about the side stage, her eyes darted back to me. They were all big and round, like maybe something had clicked for her too.

But a moment later, she looked away again.

"Nope. I don't have time to watch the concerts. Anyway, I...I heard the band was overrated."

Overrated?

"Are you sure?" I asked. "Because I…I mean they…I mean, I heard they were okay. Pretty good, actually. That's just what I heard."

It must've been someone else I'd seen. Still. She looked so familiar.

I took off my hat. "I'm Randy, by the way. Ms. Alverson told me about you. You're Flor, right?" I held out my hand.

She looked at it a long time before shaking it.

"Flor," she finally agreed, barely unclenching her jaw.

"*Flor*," I repeated in my *You Can Speak Spanish* voice. "Flower."

"No. Just Flor."

"Just Flor. Sorry."

Something had gone wrong, but I didn't know what. I didn't know *when*. A few seconds earlier, we were having a completely normal conversation, and now she looked like she couldn't stand looking at me. Like if she were a goat, she'd ram me right over the wire fence.

I chewed the edge of my thumbnail. If I had been singing and I needed to warm up the audience, I would've invited someone onstage with me. That always got a big cheer. Or maybe I'd flip my hat into the air and catch it on my fingertip. But offstage, in the petting zoo, there weren't any tricks for making someone like me. The real me, I mean.

You can't make everyone like you. Ronnie's voice drifted into my thoughts like an old song.

But just like always, I couldn't let it go. I *had* to make her like me. I had to keep trying.

"So, this is your zoo?"

"My family's." Flor scooped Chivo up and held him across her arm, rubbing his head as if he were a puppy.

"Have you been with the carnival very long?"

She narrowed her eyes. "Why do you want to know?"

I put my hat back on. "Well, it's just that we're with the carnival too. My family, I mean. We have an act—a musical act. But we're new here, and I thought you could maybe show me around?"

She set Chivo on the wood shavings next to a girl with yellow braids who was pouring water into a dish. She was the one who had sold me the bag of food. Chivo stretched his neck to sniff her fingers. For such a small animal, he sure had a big appetite.

"Go on," said a man raking out straw on the other end of the animal pen. Flor's dad, I guessed. "It's quiet around here. I can manage. Plus, I have help." The girl with the braids stood and smiled. "Go. Have fun."

Instead, Flor took a metal comb that had been resting on one of the fence posts and started brushing wood chips out of the sheep's wool. "No," she said, more to me than to him. "It'll start picking up around here soon. It always does."

You can't take it personally, I tried to remind myself. *You can't make everyone like you.*

51

I brushed off my skirt and turned to go.

"Well, it was nice to meet you anyway." I bent down to pat Chivo on the head. "Adios, Chivo. Good-bye."

Mom had said to be back at the motor home by five thirty to get ready for the big main-stage show. That meant I still had three hours to myself. I wasn't sure where to go next until my rumbling stomach suggested lunch. Except for those two mouthfuls of Junior's cold Spaghetti-Os, I hadn't eaten since breakfast.

Just past the lemonade stand was funnel cake, and a little farther on, corn on the cob. Then onion rings, then garlic fries, then deep-fried Twinkies. There were too many choices to pick just one, but not enough quarters still jangling around my pocket to try everything.

Dad would have decided for me if he had been there. He always had a plan, even when it came to lunch, and I almost never got a say in it. He would have chosen where we ate, and maybe even what we ordered. Now that I finally had the chance to decide for myself, to do whatever *I* wanted, well, I couldn't decide whether what I wanted was a churro or cheese fries. Or something else altogether. I stopped at an information booth and took a map—*Your Guide to the Dinuba Cantaloupe Fair*—hoping something would catch my eye.

What caught my eye instead was a gigantic pink gorilla.

It was almost as tall as the boy standing next to it and twice as wide. He was licking a drop of nacho cheese off his thumb.

The boy, I mean. Not the gorilla.

And nachos, I realized right then, were exactly what I wanted.

"Hi!" I said, walking toward him. "Where'd that come from?"

He looked around like maybe I was talking to someone else. "Me?" He had light brown hair that fell in a straight line, as straight as Junior's guitar strings, over his eyebrows. He wore a red-striped polo shirt and plaid shorts and sneakers with no socks.

"Well, I wasn't talking to the gorilla. Where did you get that?"

He tilted his head. "Did your mom and dad give you some spending money or something?"

I patted my pocket. "A little."

He pulled one more cheesy corn chip out of the paper tray and popped it into his mouth. Then he chucked the rest straight into a trash bin.

"Good," he said. "I'll even show you the trick to winning."

"Winning?"

"Sure. Anyone can do it. I bet you get it on your first try."

"My first try?"

"Yeah, it's easy." He picked up the gorilla. "You want to win one of these, right?"

Just picturing us trying to stuff that thing into Wicked Wanda made me laugh. I wasn't sure it would have even fit through the door. "No, I didn't mean—"

"Oh, you want a different color? That's okay, they have all different colors: blue, purple, yellow. Teddy bears too. Whatever you want. You like unicorns? They have unicorns."

I shook my head. "No. Listen, what I actually wanted to know was where you got the nachos."

He glanced over at the trash bin like he was wondering whether he should just pull the tray out again and give it to me. Like it might be easier that way. Then he looked back at me and smiled. He had figured something out.

"No problem," he said. "Water Gun Derby, then nachos. I'm Mikey, nice to meet you. Let's go."

He lifted the gorilla over his head and took off into the blinking, buzzing, bustling midway.

"No, wait, I don't want..." But it was too late. He wasn't turning back. It was either go after him or find the nachos on my own. So I trotted off, following the bobbing pink gorilla as Mikey wove through the crowd. Around us, milk-bottle pyramids clattered down as people hurled softballs into them. Lights flashed as basketballs swished through hoops. Little kids cried for balloons or face paint or caramel apples. A man with a mustache said he could guess my weight within three pounds. "Just five dollars, little lady, step right up."

Finally, Mikey stopped in front of another game, Water Gun Derby. Giant gorillas and bears and unicorns in every color, just like he'd promised, hung from the top of the booth. Under them was a countertop with squirt guns, numbered one through eight.

Inside the booth, the game operator leaned against a miniature racetrack with eight plastic horses ridden by eight tiny jockeys. Customers sat on stools behind each water gun and aimed at targets hanging a few feet away. "On your mark!" the operator shouted. "Get set!" He looked around. The players held their breath. "Go!" He blew an air horn.

All at once the players started shooting. Some squinted; some stood up. When the water hit the targets just right, the little racehorses inched forward.

"Looks like Number Seven is in the lead," the operator said. "Oh, but look out for Number Four, coming up from behind. Hurry, folks, time is running out."

The players kept squirting. A couple of them stuck their tongues out like Junior did when he was really concentrating on a chord.

"Just ten seconds left... Now eight!"

I stood on my tiptoes to watch. I counted down with the rest of the crowd. If that was what it felt like to be part of an audience, it was almost as good as being onstage.

Six! Five! Four! The racehorses wobbled forward. *Three! Two! One!* We got down to zero, and the air horn blared again.

"That's it, folks," the operator said. "Better luck next time." Everyone groaned, including me. None of the horses had crossed the finish line. The player who came closest got a consolation prize: a stuffed penguin wearing sunglasses and a tropical shirt.

Mikey shook his head. "Pitiful. No technique. See, there's a secret to winning. You want to hear it?" Before I could answer, he whispered, "It's easy. You aim just *above* the target, not right at it. Optical illusion kind of thing. Works every time. Now, come on, try it yourself."

He steered me toward seat number five. All the excitement— the cheering, the chanting, the laughing, the prizes—made me forget about my empty stomach. As breathless as I was, you would have thought it had been a real race and I had just run it. I dug into my pocket and started counting out two dollars' worth of quarters to pay for a round of Water Gun Derby.

But just as I was about to slide them across the counter to the game operator, someone reached out and pulled on my sleeve.

"Don't waste your money." It was the girl from the petting

zoo. Flor. "Let me guess. He's trying to tell you there's a secret? Trust me, the secret to winning on the midway is knowing that nothing is as easy as it looks."

Mikey elbowed her in the ribs. "Hey! Come on, Flor. She was just about to play."

"Then I got here just in time," she said. "You'll thank me later."

Flor

(2:45 P.M.)

Johnny Bean, Mikey and Maria's big brother, was working the Water Gun Derby that day. He had just turned seventeen, and it was the first summer Mr. Barsetti had let him run his own booth. He scowled impatiently at Mikey and me as Randy's hand hovered over her quarters and she tried to decide whether to play.

"*Flor*," Mikey whispered through his teeth.

Letting her play would have kept her occupied, which was exactly what I wanted. Only, it was a little risky too. What if I lost her again in the crowd? What if she spent all her money, got mad, and went right back to her family? No. I was going to have to take charge somehow.

"Are you kids coming or going?" Johnny asked. Like he didn't know either of us, like he was ten years older instead of just six. "People are waiting. The race is about to start."

Every seat except number five was taken. Another girl stood right next to it, ready to jump in if Randy gave up the spot. But Randy wasn't moving yet. She glanced up at the stuffed animals, beady-eyed and neon-furred, swaying from a cord stretched across the top of the booth.

"Well?" Johnny said again, drumming his fingers on the counter.

It was just like I told Betabel: Now or never. I swallowed and said, "Going."

"What?" Mikey and Randy both looked at me.

I cleared my throat and tried to say it louder. "Going. I mean, we should go. Come on." I dropped my chin to my chest, grabbed both of them by the wrists, and pulled. Mikey barely had time to reach back for that giant pink gorilla he always had with him. He glared at me, annoyed I had cost him the fifty cents Johnny would have given him for reeling in a new customer.

Someone bumped into Randy, knocking off her baseball cap, as we shouldered through the knot of people gathered around the game.

"No! Wait!" She froze, hands on her head, eyes darting frantically left and right as she tried to find where it had landed.

Mikey ducked down and scooped the hat up off the grass. "Got it."

I led us out to where the crowd was thinner, and we leaned against the side of a pizza stand. It smelled like basil and garlic and warm bread.

Mikey passed Randy the hat. "The Outlaws?"

"Thanks." She smoothed her hair back with her hand and put it on. "They're minor league. From where I'm from," she said quickly and quietly. "It sort of reminds me of home and how far we've come. And since I don't know when we'll go back there…" We waited a few seconds for her to finish the sentence, but she never did.

Still, Mikey didn't look away. He studied Randy's face until his eyes opened all big and round and cartoony as he finally recognized her. See, sometimes, when he was trying to find contestants for the carnival games, Mikey and his gorilla came along with me to the Family Side Stage.

"Oh, hey!" he said. "You're from—hey, *ow!*"

Tricking Miranda into missing her show would be harder if she knew that *we* knew who she was, so I pinched the back of Mikey's elbow to stop him from giving it away. Just hard enough to get his attention.

"Sorry," I said. "Thought I saw a spider."

Mikey rubbed his arm, glaring at me again, only this time looking more confused than angry about it. He didn't say anything else, though. He might not have known exactly why, but he knew I wanted him to keep quiet. It's like I said, we looked out for each other.

"Mikey, this is Randy. She's with the carnival. Her family's new here, so I'm showing her around."

"I thought you said you were too busy."

"Well...I...changed my mind. Anyway, this is Mikey. He's with the carnival too."

"We met," Randy said, holding out her hand to him. "Sort of."

"And," I continued, "he's just mad at me because if you had actually played that squirt gun game, he would have made fifty cents. And that's not counting what he gets for dragging the gorilla everywhere he goes."

Joe Ochoa—he's the games manager—he would pay us five dollars a day just to carry those giant stuffed animals around. It made people think, if some *kid* could win a big prize like that, well then, anybody could. Then they'd come and play and find out that nothing was as simple as it looked.

For two Saturdays in a row, I lugged around a green alligator so big I could have used it as a mattress. That was just so I could chip in for Lexanne's graduation present. Most of the time, I didn't think Joe's offer was worth the trouble, all those strangers pointing and staring at me wherever I went. Mikey, though, he was always saving up to buy something, so he had that gorilla with him almost all the time.

Johnny gave him another fifty cents for each customer he brought over to his booth—the top-selling game at the end of every carnival always got a bonus from Mr. Barsetti.

"You were trying to trick me?" Miranda pulled her hand back and put it on her hip.

"I didn't trick you," Mikey insisted, placing the gorilla in front of him like a shield. "You *wanted* to play, didn't you? Anyway, I didn't know you were—" He looked at me before he continued. "I didn't know you were with the carnival. Otherwise, I wouldn't have wasted all that time."

"Wasted *your* time?" Randy took a step toward him.

"Don't worry, Mikey," I interrupted. "We'll help you find someone else."

You would have thought it was easy—the last afternoon of the fair was always so busy. But the thing about it was, being at the midway was a little like being inside a kaleidoscope of strollers, tank tops, sunglasses, snow cones, water bottles, popcorn, and cotton candy—all mixed up and always moving. You had to pay attention to see faces instead of a crowd, to hear words instead of noise. To pick out just the right person. It was a good thing I knew how to pay attention.

I looked around. "There."

A family drifted between the booths. One of the kids, a little younger than us probably, had a stuffed orange python with shiny silver stripes draped over her shoulders, almost dragging on the ground. The other kid, the smaller one, dawdled behind. He didn't have a snake of his own and paused in front of every game, staring hungrily up at the prizes.

The parents stopped at a bench across from where we were standing. They unfolded a map.

"Yes." Mikey nodded.

"See? I told you."

Randy watched them too, but she didn't see what we saw. "Is one of you going to tell me what we're looking at, or what?"

I jerked my chin toward the smaller kid. "See how tired he is, how bad he wants a big prize like his sister's?" The boy climbed on the bench. He rested his elbows on his knees and his chin in his hands. One of his tube socks was slouching down around his ankle. "If he sees the gorilla, he will want it. And if he wants it, he will whine for it. And the only way to get him to stop whining is to win the prize. And the only way to win the prize—"

"Is to play the game," Mikey finished. He was already lifting the gorilla over his head.

Randy scrunched her eyebrows. "So you're just going to walk over there and hope he sees you?"

"He'll see me."

"Good luck," I said.

"Wait." Randy stepped in front of him. "Let me try."

Mikey put the gorilla down. "Are you serious? You don't even know what to do."

"You just told me what to do. How hard can it be?" she

said, grabbing a handful of the gorilla's pink hair. "Come on. Before they get up and start walking again."

Mikey looked at me, and I shrugged. She had a point.

He wasn't convinced, though. "I don't know."

"You can keep the money. I just want to see if I can do it."

"Fine. But don't be too obvious about it, okay? I don't want to lose another customer. All you have to do is just let the kid see you."

The corners of her eyes crinkled as she smiled and sauntered off with the gorilla in a one-armed stranglehold. Mikey and I put our hands to our foreheads, shielding our eyes from the sun, and watched.

Miranda strode past the family and back into the noise of the midway games. Then she spun on her toe like a ballerina and doubled back, this time more slowly, like she just happened to be walking through, browsing the sunglasses at a concession stand, considering the menu at the pretzel cart.

Finally, a few feet away from the family, she stopped, winked at us, and set the gorilla down so that it was facing the little boy. She dipped her hand into her pocket, scattered a handful of quarters on the ground, and shouted, "Whoops!"

Then she knelt down to pick them up. It was like everyone on the midway was her audience.

"So why'd you pinch me for, anyway?"

Mikey had been my first friend at the carnival. Maybe my first friend ever, if I was telling the truth about it. When we first joined Barsetti & Son, I never left the petting zoo or our RV. But Maria kept showing up to play with the animals, and Mikey kept showing up to bring her back to their RV at the end of the day. And after a while, he started coming on his own.

Later, when I mentioned I wanted to train Betabel, he didn't laugh or tell me it was a dumb idea. He went out and brought me his old skateboard.

I told him what I had overheard. How Mr. Barsetti was giving Miranda y los Reyes a chance to perform on the main stage. How Randy's dad wanted them to sing up there permanently, how he had asked for a raise and threatened to leave if they didn't get one. How the only way Mr. Barsetti could pay them more was if he kicked someone else off the show. Maybe us.

"Mr. Barsetti wouldn't do that."

"He retires games that aren't popular anymore, doesn't he? And he got rid of the Salad Wagon after no one ate there." I lowered my voice. I was not sure I wanted to say the next words out loud. "Plus, he said it might be time to make some changes. He said Rancho Maldonado isn't bringing in crowds like it used to."

Mikey sucked in a big breath of air through his teeth. "So what are you planning to do?"

When I had recognized Randy at the petting zoo, all I'd wanted was for her to get away from me and Dad and the animals—and everything else I cared about. As fast as possible. Seeing her there, feeding Chivo, and knowing she could ruin everything for us, had made my hands start to shake.

But later, after she left, I started wondering what would happen if she had a bad show instead of a great one. I imagined what might happen if she didn't sing at all. Mr. Barsetti wouldn't give them another chance like this one, not for a long time. He would probably be relieved that he could keep the Reyes family on the show without spending any more money. I could almost hear him: "Looks like she's not quite ready for the main stage. But don't worry, Reyes, those kids of yours still have a real future with Barsetti and Son."

And maybe he would forget what he said about it being time to make some changes.

That's when I followed Randy onto the midway. I went looking for Mikey first, to see if he would help me. It was just good luck that she happened to be standing right next to him and that neon-pink gorilla.

My plan was simple: Keep her busy, keep her distracted. Keep her off the main stage, whatever it took.

"I have to stop her from singing."

"She's good," Mikey said. "Like she could be a professional, almost."

I slid down against the red-green-and-white-painted side of the pizza booth. "I know." But he didn't mean *just* Randy's voice.

She had rolled one of her quarters right in front of the boy's swinging legs.

"Excuse me? I dropped my quarter. Can you get it for me?"

The boy hopped off the bench, picked up the quarter, and brought it back to Randy—and the gorilla, which she had positioned right in his path. She lifted one of its furry arms and waved it. "Gracias. Thank you," she said, her voice deep and mumbly like she had a mouthful of marbles.

She held the gorilla's hand up for the boy to slap. And he did.

"Almost," Mikey muttered. "Any second now."

Then it happened, just like we both knew it would.

"Mom! Dad!" the kid yelled, arms around the gorilla's neck. It was taller than he was. He almost couldn't lift it. "I want one!"

The parents looked up from their map. Randy flashed a perfect side-stage smile.

"Please, Mom?"

The boy took the gorilla by the arms and danced with it. He teased the hair on its head into three tall spikes. There was no way he would let his family leave the fair without one, even if it meant they had to spend the rest of their day, not to mention the rest of their money, at the Water Gun Derby.

Randy stepped over to the parents. She took off her hat. She waved it in the direction of the Water Gun Derby.

"Tell them Mikey sent you!" she called out as they folded

up their map and started walking toward the games. She picked up the gorilla and skipped back over to us, cheeks pink, eyes gleaming. She dropped the gorilla at Mikey's feet and took a bow.

I felt like we should clap.

Mikey did.

"That was unbelievable!" he said. "Hey, it's not that late. I bet Joe would still hire you to carry another one of these around for the rest of the day. We could work together to help Johnny win the bonus."

That hadn't been part of my plan, but it could still work. If Mikey kept Randy busy enough, maybe she would be late to the main-stage show. Maybe she wouldn't have enough time to practice. Maybe she would have so much fun she wouldn't even want to go back.

"Maybe some other time," she said. "All I want right now is something to eat. Nachos, remember? You promised."

That was an even better idea. "I can take you!"

I knew where to find enough sugar, oil, syrup, and salt on the fairgrounds to curdle even the strongest stomach, and hers wasn't used to fair food. It wasn't like I wanted to get her *very* sick, you know? Just too sick to sing.

"Are you sure? You don't have to go help your dad?"

"Yeah, Flor," Mikey said, winking at me. "Are you sure?"

With the sun still so high and bright, the pizza stand's shadow gave us only a skinny strip of shade to stand in. Beads of sweat tickled my nose, and I swiped them off with the back of my hand. Over at the petting zoo, Chivo and Cricket were probably climbing a stack of hay bales. They loved to climb. Papá might have been combing the sheep. Betabel would be rolling her beach ball around the shed. Rancho Maldonado was their home. It was my home. Miranda could find another stage to sing on, but the fair was the only place I belonged.

I was sure.

"Have you tried the deep-fried pickles yet?"

Miranda

(3:15 P.M.)

Every spring when we played the national anthem at Outlaw Stadium, we always got to stay and watch the game. For free. One time they even gave us all a baseball cap. Everything else cost money, though. More money than it was worth, according to Mom and Dad.

We watched other kids eat hot dogs, slurp Slushees, and squirt mustard onto their warm salted pretzels, and we didn't even waste our time wishing we could have some too. We knew what the answer would be if we asked: "*How* much? For a *hot dog*? Wait till we get home—I'll make you *six* hot dogs for that price." Instead, Mom snuck in water bottles and little bags of potato chips. *Maaaybe* some Pelon Pelo Rico candy, but only if we had just been to the Mexican grocery store that day. This one time, when Ronnie complained about how we never got to eat Cracker Jack like in the song, Mom snuck in a bag of microwave popcorn. She had a real big purse.

All our extra money went back into the band. We needed money for costumes—for the cowboy hats we special ordered, and for the vests we made ourselves, sitting around the table with a BeDazzler and a sparkling pile of rhinestones. We needed money to buy strings for Junior's bass guitar and a new accordion for Ronnie when Dad said it was time she had something more professional. And then, when Dad decided the only way we'd get more exposure was to leave home and hit the road, we needed money to buy Wicked Wanda.

Anyway, we knew better than to ask for treats at the ball-park.

But last year, during the sixth inning, when I couldn't even see what was happening on the field because the sun was shining right in my face, a vendor walked up and down the aisles with a big metal box strapped to his chest. "Churros!" he called. "Warm churros! Four dollars! Churros here."

Normally, I would've ignored him. This time, though, some lady one row down raised her hand to order one. The vendor walked over and stood there, right next to me, in a cloud of cinnamon-sugar. I couldn't help myself. My parents would've said no if I asked. So I didn't. My arm shot up to order one too. It wasn't that I didn't understand everything

Dad was always saying about sacrifice. It was just that always sticking with his plan, never doing what *I* wanted, felt like wearing a jacket that was too tight.

The vendor opened the metal box and handed me a churro so hot it warmed my fingers through the waxed-paper wrapper.

"That'll be four dollars, please."

I tapped Dad's shoulder. "Four dollars," I said, wearing my best stage smile, sweeter than the sugar I could already taste.

Dad looked startled. He started to say no. But I was holding the churro and everything, so he didn't have much choice but to reach for his wallet.

When Ronnie and Junior saw, they threw down their potato chips. "I'll take one," Junior said, reaching over Dad. "And me," said Ronnie.

The vendor started opening the box again, but Dad was back in control of the situation. "No. Just the one. We can share it."

"Four dollars," he grumbled, folding the change back into his wallet. "For a doughnut."

I broke off pieces for Mom and Ronnie and Junior, and licked off the cinnamon and sugar that stuck to my fingers.

I tore off a piece for Dad, but he waved my hand away and twisted the cap off a warm bottle of water from Mom's purse. "No, mija," he said. He ruffled my hair. He chuckled. "It's yours. You eat it."

So now I felt sorta bad about having a whole churro to

myself—cream-filled because Flor said those were best—
except I couldn't stop to even taste it, not if I wanted to keep
up with her.

"Milk shakes next? They're so thick you can't drink them
through a straw. You need a spoon. You should try the peanut
butter–chocolate. Come on." She didn't wait for an answer.
She just started walking.

We had left Mikey and the pink gorilla back at the games.
He had already eaten lunch and anyway, he was still trying to
help his big brother win that bonus. "I only have nine dollars
left since I bought that animal food at your zoo," I'd told her.
"Will that be enough?"

"*Feed*," she had said. "We call it feed. But that doesn't matter. You won't need any money."

"I won't?"

"We're family at Barsetti and Son. We look out for one
another."

She was right. Before long, and without spending even one
more quarter, I had the churro in one hand, and in the other,
an extra-thick peanut butter and chocolate shake, plus a paper
bag of candied almonds that I clung to with my pinky.

"What about the nachos?" I called out.

She was too far ahead to hear me, though, and all I could
do was follow her deeper into the Food Pavilion. Flor seemed to
know exactly where she was going, but I was lost. Completely.

Dad had researched Barsetti & Son way before we signed

on, before the show even came to our town. He told us it wasn't the biggest carnival company in California, but it was the best. Mr. Barsetti had carnivals in more cities than anyone else in the business, and he kept things running all year round.

Chasing after Flor, I couldn't even imagine what a bigger carnival might be like. She and I had stopped at four different food booths and walked past at least fifteen more by the time I gave up and stopped counting.

When I finally caught up to her, she was standing in line at the deep-fried pickle booth.

"Do you want them with plain ranch dressing or Cajun?" she asked. I had already told her I didn't really like pickles to begin with, but she insisted I had to try them. "Maybe you should try the Cajun. It's extra spicy."

"Plain, I guess?"

"Are you sure? Because Cajun is their specialty."

"Well, okay. I mean, if it's their specialty."

We made it up to the order window and Flor tapped on the screen. "Gabby? Are you in there?"

A woman with white-blond hair tied back with a pink bandanna pulled open the screen and leaned out. "Is that Flor I hear?"

Flor stepped back. "Oh! Paula. Are you working pickles now?"

"Just for a couple of hours. Gabby's had a toothache for weeks, you know. She found a dentist here in Dinuba who agreed to open up on the weekend, so I told her I'd cover her shift. How's your daddy?"

It was the same conversation we'd had at every food cart and snack hut before this one. I almost knew it by heart. The cashier would ask how Flor's dad was doing. Flor would say he was fine. The cashier would finally notice me.

"And who's this?"

"I'm Randy," I said, standing on tiptoe to wave at Paula through the window.

"She's new," Flor said. "She's with us." It was all she had to say.

"You girls hungry?"

Flor nodded.

"Hmm." Paula looked us over, taking in the churro and milk shake in my arms and the banana split in Flor's. I didn't know what else to do but smile back at her.

"It looks to me like you've found plenty to eat already," she said. "And like you started with dessert."

Flor's cheeks turned pink. "Please, Paula?" She was talking into the ground. "I really want Randy to try the pickles."

"Well..." She looked up at the ceiling, pretending to think about it. "All right. You've twisted my arm. What're you having?"

Flor looked up again, smiling. "One order of deep-fried pickles with spicy Cajun ranch, please." She stopped and turned to me. "Wait, should we get a double order?"

"A double order?" Paula and I said together.

"Just one, please," I said. "That's enough for me."

Paula dipped a slotted spoon into a big glass jar of dill pickle slices and pulled out a scoopful. She shook off the juice, then dropped the pickles into a tray of thick yellow batter. Finally, she dunked them into the deep fryer, and hot oil sizzled all around them.

I was beginning to think my brother and sister and I were missing out on more than just baseball stadium hot dogs and a pet goldfish. Flor seemed to know just about everyone at the carnival. And they knew her. They liked her.

A few people in the audience recognized me every weekend. But they didn't *know* me know me. Not like this.

Paula pulled the pickles out of the fryer a minute or two later and shook them, all toasted brown and steaming, into a cardboard tray.

"One order of deep-fried pickles," she said before squeezing a drizzle of creamy orange sauce over the top, "with spicy Cajun dressing." She passed the tray through the window. "Now, scram." She winked. "I have paying customers to serve."

I almost tipped the tray over trying to balance it in the same hand as the churro.

"That was a close one. If I get grease stains all over my skirt, I won't have anything to wear later."

Flor paused for the first time since we'd started our food run. "We'd better be careful, then. Let's go."

"Hey," I called, scampering after her. "Don't you think we should stop for a minute and maybe eat some of this?"

She didn't slow down. She didn't look back. "I thought you wanted nachos."

The nachos at Carolina's Cantina came in a plastic bucket. A big red bucket of chips, with scoops of sour cream, a dribble of salsa, piles of tomato, chunks of chicken, globs of guacamole— and nacho cheese oozing all over everything.

If we didn't find someplace to stop and sit, I was going to be performing in a nacho-covered skirt. Even Flor looked like she needed a break, only every seat on the covered patio outside Carolina's was taken. Flor stood right in the middle of the tables and turned around and around in slow circles, looking as lost as I'd felt a few minutes earlier. "Maybe we can just... sit on the ground?"

But Carolina's Cantina was basically an outdoor taquería, and I knew taquerías.

I put my hand on Flor's shoulder to stop her spinning. "I got this. We aren't going to sit on the ground. Just be ready to move."

Flor's mistake was looking at the tables. What you had to do was look at the plates. "Now!"

I almost dropped the churro leaping to a table where a woman was chewing her last bite of taquito and wiping a smudge of avocado from the corner of her mouth. The woman sitting on the other side of the table shook her cup. Nothing left inside but ice cubes.

"Excuse me?"

Flor stood behind me and whisper-hissed in my ear. "Stop! They're still eating."

But if we waited around for them to finish, someone else would snap up the table first.

"Excuse me?" I said again. "Are you leaving?"

The women looked at each other. The one with the taquito swallowed. "We were just finishing up, as a matter of fact. Would you girls like the table?"

I set my milk shake down in reply, and the women started clearing their plates.

"Sorry about that," Flor mumbled as they walked away. "Thank you for the table, though."

We arranged the food between us: The banana split was quickly melting into ice cream soup, the cherry half buried under a drooping tower of whipped cream. Both churros were squished in the middle where we had been holding on to them. Cream was oozing out of mine. Then there were the almonds, the shakes, the nachos, the pickles.

"Where should we start?" Flor asked. "Did you want to try the pickles first?"

But I had already cleared a space in front of me for the bucket.

"It's flawless," I murmured.

"It's nachos," said Flor.

She didn't understand. She couldn't.

Usually by the time the nachos got to me, the only chips left were the ones without any cheese on them. Or else the sour cream was all runny and the guacamole had turned brown.

These were practically gourmet. I almost hated to disturb a single chip. Almost. I pulled one, smothered in cheese, from the middle of the bucket, then used another chip to top it with some chicken, a tomato cube, and a little avocado. A perfect bite. And then another.

Next, I reached for the churro, stopped for a spoonful of milk shake, then finally moved on to a slice of deep-fried pickle.

It was crispy on the outside and tangy in the middle. The Cajun ranch was spicy, but nothing compared to the salsa I was used to eating. "Not bad." I popped a second into my mouth.

It took me a while to notice when Flor had stopped eating. She was just swirling her spoon around the ice cream puddle. "What are you humming?" she asked.

I hadn't noticed I was humming either. "Oh, it's just this song we made up, my brother and my sister and me. It's really good. I was hoping we could sing it in our act. Only, our dad, well, he won't let us. But if he would just *listen*..."

"You don't get to pick your own music?"

"Dad has a plan." I shrugged and ate another pickle. "What about your dad? Does he let you try new things at the zoo?"

She twirled the ends of her hair around a finger. "It depends. We have this pig I'm trying to train. That's new, and he doesn't seem to mind. Or even notice." She sighed. "Sometimes I think we'd be better off if he *did* have a plan."

Then she dropped her spoon. "How are you still eating? Are you sure you've never had fair food before?"

Maybe I should have paced myself, but it was the first time in weeks that my food hadn't come out of a microwave or a can, or both.

"Tough stomach," I said, crunching on another pickle. I pushed the tray over to Flor. "You better take these before I eat them all."

Miranda y los Reyes played a lot of quinceañeras and a lot of Taco Tuesdays. We booked baptisms and retirement parties too, and, once in a while, a wedding.

It was good word of mouth, Dad always said. Good exposure. That's how you build an audience.

"They always give you food at the end," I told Flor. "Only it's always the leftovers."

Enchiladas after they had been sitting in a warming tray for hours so the cheese had turned all rubbery. Or albondigas when all that was left in the pot was just some onion and carrot floating in broth—no more meatballs. The burned bottom layer of a dish of rice.

"Whatever they give us, Dad says, 'Fill up. This is dinner.'"
I licked Cajun ranch dressing off my fingers. "You're lucky. You
get to come out here every day? We're always too busy."

Flor sat up straighter. "We're busy too, you know. This is just
a quiet day, that's all. Maybe it's because one of the main-stage
acts canceled and no one's ever heard of the replacement."

My last drink of milk shake went down harder than all
the rest. "I didn't mean you weren't busy. Just that I wish I
came out here more often."

Flor relaxed, leaned back in her chair, and covered what
was left of the pickles with a napkin. "Sorry."

"You're not going to eat those?"

She slid the tray back over to me.

Flor

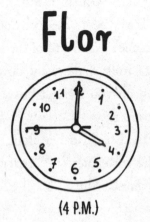

(4 P.M.)

The line was long, but it always moved fast. Randy didn't know that, though.

"If you don't feel like waiting, we can just find something else," I offered.

Something slower, I thought, and *not so spinny*. Like the carousel or even the kiddie coaster.

Randy gazed up at the sign above the Gravitron. DEFY GRAVITY! it dared above an airbrushed painting of two space-ships locked in battle, firing lasers across a purple-black sky. EXPERIENCE THE POWER OF CENTRIFUGAL FORCE!

The Gravitron was a good ride. It was probably one of the best in the whole carnival. But just the thought of being whipped around in circles after everything we had eaten put a sour-sick taste at the back of my throat.

"You might think it's boring."

The milk shake, churro, and nachos combination should have been enough to make her queasy at least. But even after the deep-fried pickles, she was bouncing on the balls of her feet like she could've topped it all off with a bacon-wrapped Twinkie and a plate of Tater Twists.

When I had told her we would get on some rides after lunch, it seemed like a good idea, right in line with my plan. If the food didn't make her sick, the Gravitron would. Now I wasn't so sure *my* stomach could handle it. And I wasn't sure hers couldn't.

Randy stood on tiptoe to try to peek inside the Gravitron. It was one of the older rides. "Only one on the West Coast!" Mr. Barsetti used to brag. But he was always saying that kind of thing. "Friendliest petting zoo this side of the Rockies," I'd heard him tell people about Rancho Maldonado. "Sweetest lemonade in the state!" It made me wonder if anyone was actually keeping track.

The Gravitron was dull silver and shaped like a flying saucer. At night, bands of red lights raced up and down its sides. Every few minutes, the doors slid open and thumping dance-party music poured out. Riders stumbled off, straightening their glasses, tucking their shirts back in, taming flyaway strands of hair. When they had all filed out, another group of riders would step aboard. The doors would clatter shut so we couldn't hear the music anymore, just a few muffled screams that slipped through as the Gravitron began to spin.

Randy chewed on her thumbnail. She dropped her heels to the ground. "Let's do it."

I clutched my stomach and followed her into line behind four girls about our age. They wore matching blue jerseys like they had come to the festival straight from a game or from practice or something. One sat on top of the railing and braided another one's ponytail. They passed around a cone of cotton candy, each one pulling off a chunk of pink floss. Being part of the carnival was the closest I had ever come to being part of a team. Otherwise, I didn't belong to anything the way those girls belonged to one another.

"Do you ever miss it?" Randy asked, still gnawing on her fingernails.

"Miss what?"

She pulled her hand out of her mouth and held it behind her back. "Having friends. Being normal."

I crossed my arms. "Mikey's my friend. And Maria. Libby was too, before she left. Then there's Johnny and Lexanne. They're older, but they're still friends. *We're* all normal."

"But, I mean, going to school. I miss school. I miss knowing everyone. I miss how it was when everyone wasn't a stranger."

Maybe we wouldn't be strangers anymore if the Reyes family left their motor home and actually talked to us once in a while. Maybe their dad wouldn't have been so quick to tell Mr. Barsetti to drop us from the lineup. But I didn't say so out loud.

The Gravitron stopped. Riders stepped off, rumpled and ruffled. Riders stepped on, antsy and anxious. The line lumbered forward. Deb was at the front of it, taking tickets. She had a clear blue visor that cast a blue-tinged half-moon shadow over her freckled nose.

"Well, hello there, Ms. Flor. It's been a while since you came around to see me. Where've you been?"

"Helping my papá mostly. Since Mamá started that new job."

She nodded slowly. "That's right. Yes, that's right." Deb was tall; I barely came up to her shoulder. She had been a professional volleyball player before she came to the carnival. She was always offering to keep an eye on us kids after closing time if the carnival parents wanted to have a date night. They were usually too tired, though. "And who's this? New friend? It's about time."

Randy stepped out from behind me and waved.

"She's new to the carnival," I said. "But she hasn't been on any of the rides yet. This will be her first."

Deb touched the edge of her visor and bowed her head. "I'm honored."

"We don't have any tickets, though. Will you let us on?"

Someone behind us huffed impatiently.

Deb clicked down twice on the little counter she carried to keep track of how many spaces were left on the ride. "Get in there," she whispered. "You two have fun, all right?"

Four metal steps led up to the Gravitron's entrance. They rattled under our feet as we climbed aboard. Inside, red and white lights flashed in time with the *thump, thump, thump* that pulsed through crackly speakers.

Randy tried to tell me something, but I couldn't hear.

"Huh?"

She cupped her hands around her mouth and shouted, "There aren't any seats!"

"No seats," I agreed.

On the Gravitron, everyone stood in a circle and leaned back on black vinyl cushions. At the center of the circle was a control station where the ride operator sat. It was Marcus this time—it was almost always Marcus. He was the only one who could stand being inside the Gravitron for hours at a time. He wore headphones over his ears to muffle the music, and sunglasses to block the blue and green lights that whizzed above his head like a siren.

Sometimes, on setup nights, when the work was done and there weren't any guests yet, Marcus would bring out his guitar and sing campfire songs for all of us. He was teaching Mikey and me to play a little, even. When he saw me, he pushed his sunglasses up over his forehead and pointed at two spots next to each other.

We hurried toward them, then leaned back and waited.

"Aren't there any seat belts?"

"No seat belts either."

"So we just stand here? And it spins?"

"Pretty much."

She pressed her lips together. I couldn't tell if she was nervous or disappointed.

I'd avoided the Gravitron for months after we first joined the carnival. All that screaming coming from inside made me wonder why anyone would get on to begin with. I made excuses whenever Mikey came around to see if I wanted to get on. I said my papá needed me to rake out the pen, or that one of the animals had gotten sick. But then, the minute she was finally tall enough, Maria tried the Gravitron and said it was the best ride at the whole carnival. Maria was three years younger. If she wasn't afraid, I had to give it a try at least.

"Actually, I think you'll like it," I told Randy. Suddenly, I wanted her to like it the same way I had once wanted the kids from school to like our ranch. If they liked the ranch, then they might like me too. They might stop thinking it was weird the way I talked about animals all the time. They might want to come over even when it wasn't for a field trip. Except they never did.

My stomach, which had been woozy after all the fair food we ate, was now bubbly with nervous excitement. That was what it must feel like to have a new friend over to your house for the first time, I thought. To throw open the door to your bedroom and show off all your best things. To hope she thought it was all exactly as great as you did.

When all the spaces on the Gravitron were filled, Marcus got out of the operator's booth to pull the doors shut. Randy flinched when the latch clanged.

I used to hate that part too, when everything was about to begin and you couldn't do anything but wait for it.

Back behind the control panel, Marcus read the safety instructions. No somersaults, no backflips, no headstands, no spins. He sounded bored. He probably read those instructions more than a hundred times a day, and almost no one paid attention when he did.

"Please remain standing," he droned.

"Permanecen de pie," Randy said in that strange way she was always repeating things in Spanish. She squeezed her eyes shut. "Remain standing."

The lights went out. Everyone screamed.

"Enjoy your ride." Marcus flicked his sunglasses back over his eyes and gave me a thumbs-up. Then he flicked on a black light that made the middle of my Rancho Maldonado shirt glow purplish white.

"What's going on?" Randy's teeth were glowing too. The music blared. Every beat shot up through my toes and straight to my temples.

It was too late for me to answer. We were already spinning. A red-and-yellow starburst flashed on the ceiling. The lights whirling around Marcus's booth morphed into a blue-green blur.

The faster we spun, the louder we screamed. Our seat backs crept upward, but we didn't fall, we floated. The man next to me ignored the safety instructions and balanced on his head.

Randy's eyes were still shut, so I shook her arm. She couldn't miss this.

"Look!"

She was suspended at least a foot off the floor. That was the way the Gravitron worked. It spun around so fast, it pinned you to the wall, and for a while at least, you really could defy gravity.

Randy started screaming too. But it wasn't a scared scream. It was a laughing scream, a giddy scream, a Gravitron scream.

Once in a while, if we weren't in a hurry to get back on the road, Mr. Barsetti let us keep a ride or two open after a carnival had closed. Not very often—"soaring cost of electricity, you know"—but sometimes. And on those nights, Mikey and I always used to beg for one of the rides to be the Gravitron. When it was full of guests like this, we had to obey all the rules.

When it was just us carnival kids, though, no one cared if we climbed all the way up to the ceiling or walked sideways across the walls.

Next time, we would have to bring Randy with us. Maybe after the carnival closed that night.

Then I remembered: Whatever happened that night, we probably wouldn't come back to ride the Gravitron together. Miranda and I were not really friends. I didn't want her around. The longer she stayed, the more I had to worry.

The Gravitron began to slow. "Please return to a standing position," Marcus warned. "Your ride is coming to an end."

Everyone booed. The pressure against my shoulders eased. I slid back to the ground, a little at a time. As soon as the Gravitron bumped to a stop, the regular white lights turned back on. The music was softer now, but I could still feel it pulsing in my ears. Randy took off her hat and fanned herself with it.

"That. Was. Amazing," she said.

"I'm glad you liked it." And even though it was hard to admit, I really was.

Marcus was at the door, taking people under the elbow and helping them down, just in case they were too dizzy to get out safely on their own.

When it was our turn to go, he winked at me. Instead of guiding us off the ride, he steered us back around the circle. "One more time?" he said as the music thumped on.

I started to shake my head. But Randy jumped up from behind me. "Yes!"

Miranda

(4:15 P.M.)

My legs wobbled like strawberry jelly, and my jaw ached from screaming, and I could've stayed on the Gravitron for another ten turns.

The operator would've let us stay on, at least for a third ride. I could tell by the way he held his arm out like a challenge as we followed the other riders toward the exit. Flor must not have seen him, though. She pushed me right out the door.

For a little while, when the ride was spinning the fastest, it almost felt like being onstage, the music thumping, all of us floating, my voice getting all jumbled up with everyone else's. Junior and Ronnie would have loved it. Well, Ronnie would have pretended like she didn't. She would've complained about her hair getting tangled, or people stepping on her toes or something. But she would've loved it. She would have lined up to ride again. Dad would've never gotten on in the first place, but more than anyone, I wished he had been there. Maybe he would have seen that sometimes the best thing you can do is lean back and let go.

"Amazing," I said again and again as we stepped, blinking, back into the bright afternoon. My voice sounded far away. Hollow, and a little scratchy. I hoped it was just my ears readjusting to the quiet.

"Hey, does my voice sound weird to you?"

"Weird how?"

"I don't know," I said. I stretched open my jaw. I cleared my throat. "Like...hoarse?" I was going to have to be more careful if I wanted to have any voice left that evening.

"You're not losing your voice, are you? Was it from the screaming, do you think?" Flor looked over my shoulder, back at the Gravitron, as we walked away from it. "Maybe we should get on again, I mean if you liked it so much."

"Probably shouldn't." The words sounded sandpapery rough at their edges.

"Well, then what do you want to get on next?" she asked. "Bumper cars? Log Jammer? You don't mind getting a little bit wet, do you?"

I didn't mind at all. My head was baking under my ball cap, and any makeup still left on my face after I'd washed earlier had definitely melted down my cheeks by then. A spray of cold water would have been perfect. *Perfecto.* I looked up where Flor was pointing and watched a log-shaped boat tilt over the edge of a steep chute of fast-running water and drop.

Everyone inside screamed—it sounded like birds twittering from where we stood—as water splashed over the log.

Still. *Discipline,* I heard Dad say. *Sacrifice.* I shook my head. No more screaming. My voice needed rest. "Does anyone sell hot tea around here?" I looked around for a booth that wasn't candy-colored.

Flor wrinkled her nose. "There's always a big pot of coffee in the cafeteria tent. It's hot, but it smells like a burned-out campfire, and Mamá always says it's as thick as mud. Later on, when the sun goes down, some of the food stands will start selling hot chocolate. But no hot tea. Not in the middle of summer."

"Didn't think so." She was still thinking, though, like it really bothered her that there was something the carnival *didn't* have.

"*Iced* tea, though, I know where you can get iced tea. Any flavor you want. They sell mango iced tea at the Barbecue Pit, or passion fruit over at Paradise Grill. If you want plain iced tea, we can get that pretty much anywhere." She looked like she was about to take off again to prove it to me, so I stepped in front of her.

"No, that's all right," I whispered. I touched my throat.

"Maybe…maybe I should just go back to my motor home. But can we stop at your petting zoo on the way? I want to say good night to Chivo."

Flor looked away, but I couldn't tell what at. Her bangs had fallen in her face again. She bit her lip.

"No, you don't want to go yet," she said finally, swiping the hair out of her eyes. "It's too early. If you want to see some more animals, I know where we can find more animals. Lots more. Goats too. Let's go." She was off, leading us away from the crowded midway and toward a rectangular building near the back of the fairgrounds, right behind the side stage. The black letters painted over the entrance said EXHIBITION HALL. Flor paused, one hand on the door, and waited for me to catch up.

"We can cut through here." An air-conditioned blast blew into our faces as she pulled it open. The exhibition hall was just as packed as the midway, only inside, voices rose up and echoed against the walls so all I could hear was a low, mumbling hum. Every now and then, a snippet of conversation, like a favorite lyric, cut through the noise.

"I don't believe I've ever come across a dahlia with such a large bloom before, have you? It's the size of a pie plate!"

"Did you get to taste the strawberry-rhubarb jam? Exquisite."

"You know what I could go for right about now? Nachos."

Be sure you go to Carolina's Cantina, I wanted to tell them. *Ask for the bucket.* But I couldn't tell who had said it. The way sounds bounced against the walls in the hall, whoever it was could have been standing right next to me, or they could have been on the opposite side of the building.

We walked by a collection of quilts draped over wooden racks. One, with a red prize ribbon pinned to the corner, showed a sun setting behind craggy mountains. It looked like a painting, only it was made of fabric scraps: purples and blues and oranges and grays. On another quilt, pink-and-yellow pinwheels tumbled across a pale green background.

I ran my fingers across shelves stacked with cans of peaches, cherries, and plums. Grape jelly, strawberry jam, orange marmalade, lemon relish. I imagined one of Junior's cans of Spaghetti-Os up there and smiled. And then I realized they were all probably wondering where I was and when I'd be back.

We made our way to the far end of the building, where judges were sampling bites from five different apple pies. We didn't stay to see who won.

Instead, Flor led us through another set of doors, back outside, and onto ground that was damp and squishy. The air smelled green and...mucky.

I pinched my nose. "What *is* that?"

"Livestock," Flor said. She inhaled deeply. "But first, let's see the poultry."

Hens were clucking. I read the labels attached to their metal cages. An Orpington shook out her gold-brown feathers before settling down with a quiet cackle. Dominiques—those were black and white—scratched at the sawdust that lined the bottom of their cages.

A boy dressed all in white, except for the green scarf around his neck, lifted a rooster with silky black tail feathers out of its cage. He popped open a bottle of baby oil and rubbed a little of it on the rooster's comb and feet.

I yanked on one of Flor's sleeves. "What is he doing?"

"He's probably getting ready for showtime."

"Showtime? It's an *act*? All these people—they aren't *with* us, are they? With the carnival?" I knew I hadn't been paying close attention to what happened off the side stage, but I didn't think I could have somehow missed a traveling barnyard.

Flor opened her mouth a little, like she wasn't sure I was serious. Then she laughed.

"Hey, don't laugh!—I've never been here, remember?"

She stopped. "Sorry. No, it's not an act. It's sort of like . . . a contest. All these kids are from here, from Dinuba. They raise their animals and they bring them to the fair to compete for prizes. The oil helps make the rooster's comb all shiny. Judges look for little details like that."

Farther down, on the other side of the aisle, a girl in the same white uniform cleaned her bird with what looked like a diaper wipe. Still another girl crouched with a turkey held tight against her leg. I jumped back. Until then, the closest I had ever been to a turkey was at Thanksgiving dinner. This one was bigger and a lot more... *alive*.

"Don't worry," Flor said. "She trained it. That's part of the competition."

The girl spread out the turkey's wing, flicked away some wood shavings that clung to its feathers, and tucked the wing back in. The turkey held its head high. It gobbled like it was proud of itself. "Buena suerte," I whispered. "Good luck."

Past the chickens and turkeys were larger pens with goats and lambs. Kids reached underneath them with clippers to trim their hair. They swabbed the insides of their ears with damp washcloths. There were parents around, but they weren't working. Some were reading, or knitting, and some napped on camp chairs.

Inside one of the pens was a lamb with a baby-blue blanket spread over his back, and white gym socks on his feet.

"Look at you," I said, crouching in front of him. "Look at your little socks." I reached out to scratch his nose, but Flor put her hand in front of mine to stop me.

"I was just going to say hello."

"But look: Someone must have just finished giving this

lamb a bath. They probably wouldn't want anyone to mess with him. That's why he has the socks on—so he doesn't get all dirty again before the show."

"You sure know a lot about this stuff."

Flor dropped her head, and her bangs fell over her eyes. "You think that's weird? The kids at school used to say all I ever talked about was animals. *They* thought it was weird."

"My friends said all I ever talked about was singing. I don't think it's weird. I just think you know a lot, that's all." I stood up. "Lo siento, oveja. Sorry, sheep. Stay clean."

Then my ears caught a rumble of energy and excitement from somewhere close by.

I'd know that sound anywhere.

Applause.

"Where's that coming from?" I asked, turning in a circle. "Is there another stage back here? A concert? A magician?"

"No," Flor said. "That's the auction."

Flor

(4:30 P.M.)

According to the rules where we were living, you had to be at least eight years old to bring an animal to compete at the county fair. It felt strange remembering a time when we were just guests at the carnival. But before we joined Barsetti & Son, Mamá and Papá and I never missed the county fair, and we always went to the livestock rings when kids were showing the animals they had raised.

I couldn't wait to be one of them with a crisp white shirt and a green scarf tied under my collar—even if it meant standing out there in the middle of the ring with everybody watching me. My favorites were the beef projects. The kids would lead their calves, red-and-white Herefords and black-and-white Holsteins, around the ring by halters. Even though they were sometimes taller and always heavier, the animals obeyed, mostly, when the kids nudged their feet into place with pointy-tipped show sticks. And they stood, calm and still, heads raised high, when the judges patted their muscles.

Those kids didn't get teased for knowing everything there was to know about their animals. They didn't get laughed at when they could answer questions like *How much does this animal eat a day? Can you show us where its dewlap is? Where does sirloin come from?*

Instead, they got prizes. It wasn't like at school, not even close.

This one Sunday, when we were still living at the ranch, Papá and I found an owl pellet out in the middle of the cherry orchard. To tell the truth, Papá was the one who found it. It was just a black lump, like a dirt clod, and I would have missed it if he hadn't shown me. I brought it to school the next day and passed it around right after lunch recess.

"What *is* it?"

"It's called an owl pellet," I said, standing at the front of the class, trying to speak up the way Ms. Matsumoto was always reminding me to. "After an owl eats, everything it can't digest, like bones or fur or feathers, gets turned into one of these pellets, and the owl coughs it up."

It was one of the most interesting things I had ever seen.

"If we open it, we can find out the last thing this owl ate. Papá says there is usually a skull inside!"

Nobody gasped in excitement the way I had. No one fought over who would get to tear into the pellet first.

"You like to play with *owl puke*?"

"Ewww," they all groaned.

Things would be different when I could join those kids who raised the farm animals, I told myself.

When I was finally old enough to enter the competition, Papá and Mamá said I couldn't raise a calf after all. They said we didn't have enough room—even though we still had a barn back then and a pasture for grazing. I wondered if maybe it was because we didn't have enough money. I had started paying attention to things like that by then. The way Mamá would sew patches over the holes in my jeans instead of buying me a new pair like she used to. The way she started giving Papá haircuts at home in the kitchen. The way they both stood outside, looking gloomily up at the dark gray storm clouds that gathered over our cherry trees. Too much rain could ruin the crop.

They still let me pick out a rabbit to raise, though. I chose a New Zealand White and named her Primavera. I wrote down everything I fed her in a spiral notebook. Every day after school I changed her straw bedding and checked her ears for mites. I scrubbed stains out of her snowy coat with vinegar and warm water. I learned how to lift her out of the wood-and-wire hutch that Dad built in the backyard, and how to position her for judging. See, you don't lead a bunny around the show ring like you do the bigger animals—even though you *can* train one to walk on a leash. Instead, you set her on a mat with her legs tucked underneath so she looks just like a scoop of vanilla ice cream. I fed her apple slices when she cooperated. Apples were like candy to Primavera.

But that was the summer we joined the carnival, so I never did get to show her and win a ribbon. At least Primavera got to come along with us and be part of the petting zoo. I still snuck her apple slices sometimes.

The auction schedule was stapled to a wooden post outside the show ring. I ran my finger down the edge and stopped at 4:30. The rabbit auction was about to start. Back on the midway, when Randy said she wanted to go home, I was worried I wouldn't be able to stop her. The deep-fried pickles hadn't worked, and neither had the Gravitron. All I could do now was keep her distracted, and the animals seemed to be working.

"Do you want to watch the auction?"

"Sure," Randy said. "For a little while. But I should get back to Wanda after that."

"Wanda?"

"She's our motor home."

I nodded and hoped the auction would be exciting enough to change her mind.

We found seats near the top of creaky wooden bleachers.

Randy picked up an auction paddle someone had left behind, No. 210, and fanned herself with it.

"So how come you don't bring any of your animals out here? Chivo's sweeter than any of the goats we saw back there. He'd win all the prizes."

Chivo was no showman. He was scrawny and scruffy and would rather play hide-and-seek than follow me around a ring. But it wasn't just that.

"You have to enter in your home county. We're never in one place long enough to have one. Anyway, they don't give prizes for being sweet."

A boy carried the first rabbit to the middle of the ring.

"First up," announced the auctioneer, "is Christopher Joseph with a five-and-a-half-pound fryer."

The auctioneer's voice revved: "Let's! Start! With! Five!"

Then burned rubber: "I see five, that's five. Who's gonna show me six? Now six? Six! Now seven, looking for seven, who's gonna show me seven?"

Only, it sounded more like horseflies do when they're stuck between the screen and the window and buzzing wildly to get out.

Randy wrinkled her nose and leaned forward. "What is he even saying?"

"He's trying to make the price go higher."

The auctioneer pointed into the audience as paddles

popped up like groundhogs. "I have eight, that's eight. Now, nine. Who's gonna show me nine?"

Randy still looked confused, so I tried to explain. "A lot of times friends and family work it out beforehand who's going to bid and how much. That way, pretty much every kid gets a good price. They can use the money to buy another animal next year."

"Parents are always trying to work things out beforehand." Randy shook her head. "But maybe he could've figured it out on his own. Maybe he could've figured it out *better*."

I thought about Mamá and how she had decided for me that I should go back to school. "Yeah. Maybe."

Christopher cradled his bunny, staring straight ahead as the price rose.

"And sold!" the auctioneer announced finally. "At twenty-one dollars, a record for Dinuba. Congratulations, young man."

The bleachers rocked as the whole crowd, Randy and me included, stood up and cheered.

With everyone still clapping, Christopher left the ring, shoulders drooping. He wiped a tear off his cheek with his white shirtsleeve.

"What's the matter?" Randy asked, sitting back down. "Didn't he just set a record?"

"It's probably because the rabbit is not his anymore. Someone else bought it."

It was all part of the process. You knew it going in. Some

kids didn't even name their animals. They didn't want to get too attached before it was time to sell them.

Still, knowing you're going to lose something doesn't always make it any easier when you finally do.

A girl stepped into the ring, stroking the ears of her golden-brown Palomino.

"Next up is Lucinda Mendez with a four-pound fryer. Let's start the bidding at five, do I see five?"

An auction paddle sprouted up from the second row.

"Must be her parents," Randy said, as though she had suddenly become a junior livestock expert.

Lucinda's long, dark hair was pulled back in a braid that hung over one shoulder. She looked at her feet. She kicked some pebbles with the toe of her boot.

"We're at five, I have five," the auctioneer chanted. "Who's gonna show me six? What about six?"

People fidgeted with their paddles, but no one bid. Lucinda looked up at her parents with wide, glassy eyes. She scratched the rabbit behind its ears.

"How about five and a quarter, then? Five twenty-five, now, five twenty-five. Let me remind you folks that this is all for a good cause. Every cent goes back to the children. Five twenty-five."

Randy learned so far forward I thought she might topple over.

Lucinda's white shirt was big and blousy on her, shoulder

seams halfway to her elbows, cuffs folded over twice. Mamá used to buy all my clothes too big like that—so I wouldn't grow out of them so fast.

The green uniform scarf fluttered out behind her like a tiny cape. I remembered how badly I wanted to wear that uniform, how much I wanted to belong.

And then I just could not help it. I could not let her stand there feeling like everyone was watching and no one was on her side.

I snatched the auction paddle that Randy was holding and stood up, waving it. "Right here!"

The auctioneer pointed. "Good! I have five twenty-five, five twenty-five. Now five fifty. What about five fifty? Who's gonna show me five fifty?"

Lucinda's parents stood up and stared into the audience, trying to figure out who had raised their bid. But by then, I had sat back down and covered my face with my hand. Peeking through my fingers, I saw Lucinda's dad raise his own paddle again.

"That's five fifty, now five seventy-five." What a relief.

Just as I was starting to stand up to leave, Randy grabbed the paddle off my lap. "Six fifty!"

The auctioneer's low, steady cadence stopped short. "Six fifty?" He wiped his forehead with a handkerchief and started up again. "Looks like we skipped ahead to six fifty, folks, six fifty. Do I have six seventy-five? Someone show me six seventy-five."

I caught Randy by the elbow and pulled her back down. "What are you doing?"

She didn't answer. Lucinda's parents had raised their paddle.

"That's six seventy-five. Now, seven. How about seven?"

Randy sprang up again. "Seven!"

Lucinda smiled. She held her rabbit up a little higher.

"How about seven twenty-five?"

Lucinda's parents looked at each other. They looked at the auctioneer. They shook their heads.

"We're still at seven, I have seven. Do I see seven twenty-five? Going once, twice, and sold! That's seven dollars to Number 210, way up in back. Seven dollars to Number 210. Thank you for supporting our young people."

I took back the paddle before Randy could cause any more trouble. "We have to get out of here." I put my head down and tottered across the bleachers. Randy pranced down after me.

"What were you thinking?" I asked when we were back outside. The auctioneer had just announced the next rabbit.

"Same as you. We couldn't leave her hanging there, not when that boy before her set a *record*. Great idea, by the way."

I closed my eyes and rubbed my temples.

"But, Randy, that was a real auction. If you win, you have to pay."

Her eyes widened, and she stuck her thumbnail in her mouth. "So what do we do?"

I flipped the auction paddle over, front to back, back to front, then flipped it into a trash can. There wasn't much we *could* do. "Let's just hope whoever had this paddle likes rabbit stew, I guess. Come on."

Since we couldn't stay at the auction, I thought I could try to stop Miranda with food again. Maybe one of the Cantaloupe Fair specials like cantaloupe gazpacho or shrimp tacos with cantaloupe salsa.

"Wait, what do you mean, rabbit stew?"

"I mean, I hope they enjoy the rabbit you bought them."

"Enjoy having a new rabbit to cuddle, or..." Her black eyebrows were almost touching.

"No. Enjoy having the rabbit...for dinner. Now, we should really get out of here in case anyone noticed us."

She did not move. "They're going to *eat* the rabbit?"

"*Someone* is going to. Why do you think they called it a fryer?"

She cringed. "No."

Kids visiting the ranch always made faces like that when Dad told them we ate some of the animals. Like we'd done something terrible. It was not fair. "Where do you think your chicken nachos came from?"

She bit down on her thumbnail again. "Well, I know. But it's different. I didn't *know* that chicken."

I didn't want to admit it, but the thing of it was, I understood what she meant. If there was one good thing about never taking Primavera into the show ring, it was that no one else ever got to put her in a stew pot.

"Why can't *we* just pay for it? I still have nine dollars in quarters left." She patted her pocket, and they clinked.

"If I hadn't found you when I did, Mikey would have made sure you spent every last one at the Water Gun Derby."

She was bouncing on her toes again. "Still, it's enough, isn't it? I only bid seven."

"No, you bid seven dollars *per pound*."

She slumped.

Joe might still be willing to pay us to carry those giant stuffed animals around. But this late in the afternoon, it wouldn't be his usual fee. We could go back to the Water Gun Derby and help Mikey and Johnny. At fifty cents a customer, it would take us until closing time to even come close to earning enough—which could be exactly what I needed to stop Randy from performing. She seemed pretty serious about making sure that rabbit stayed off the menu, and to be completely honest, I sort of wanted to save him too.

But before I could tell her my plan, Randy clapped her hands in front of her nose. "Wait, I've got it. I know what to do. We have to hurry, though. It's getting late."

Miranda

(4:50 P.M.)

Lunchtime would have been better and dinner would have been best, but this would work. There were still enough people eating on the patio. Enough couples on dates, families having a snack, or friends deciding what to do next.

Everything would be fine. I hoped.

We would be out of there in half an hour—less than that. Maybe. And I'd only be a little late getting back to Wicked Wanda.

As long as the restaurant managers didn't kick us out. That was what I needed Flor for.

"I don't know," she said for about the fiftieth time, just

staring up at the Carolina's Cantina sign like we had all day. "Going out there in front of everyone? Strangers?"

"So pretend you know them like you know everyone else around here!" Flor could be just as stubborn as Dad. I took a breath and calmed my voice. "Listen," I said for the fifty-first time. "You know animals; I know singing. You don't have to get up in front of anyone. All you have to do is see if the manager will let you have an empty cup. Explain what we're trying to do, and say that if we have any money left over, we'll split it. Trust me. My brother and sister and I do this *all* the time."

"I . . . don't know."

I tapped my foot. She just stood there.

"Just *go*!" I gave her a light shove between the shoulder blades. "All you have to do is stand there. Leave the rest to me."

Finally, she took a limping step to the counter, twirling the ends of her hair around a finger.

"And see if they have some lemon wedges and a little hot water," I added, remembering my voice. If we couldn't find tea it was the next best thing.

I watched her get in line and move closer and closer toward the window. When I was certain she'd go through with it, I stuck the very edge of my thumbnail between my teeth and hummed.

It would work. Probably.

But I wasn't as sure as I'd just told Flor I was.

I was used to singing for tips. I was great at singing for tips. Singing for tips was how we saved up enough to buy Wicked Wanda so that when an opportunity came rolling into town, we were ready to roll along with it.

Only, I always had Ronnie and Junior standing right behind me. We always had Mom sitting in the audience, pointing her fingers at the corners of her mouth to remind us to smile. And we always had Dad telling us what to play. I didn't know if I could do it all without them. But I knew I had to try.

My plan was to go from table to table, taking requests. Flor would follow me with the cup, collecting change, and if everything went the way I hoped, we would earn enough to buy that rabbit before it ended up in someone's belly.

And I could get back in time to rehearse for the show that night.

"Think of it as a warm-up," I said to myself.

I closed my eyes and imagined Junior's bass and Ronnie's accordion. I even pictured Dad with his arms folded across his chest as he counted through every bar, listened for any stray note so that, later, he could make sure we practiced until it was perfect. I imagined myself singing. And then I was ready.

I opened my eyes and moved to the center of the patio so I could take a better look at everyone eating there under the red and green umbrellas.

A woman sitting by herself with a Diet Coke and a quesadilla. No.

She probably didn't want to be interrupted, and anyway, it might make her uncomfortable. Although, if she was *really* uncomfortable, she might pay me to *stop* singing. I changed the no to a maybe.

Four boys about Junior's age. Definitely no.

A couple. Matching white hair. Matching Windbreakers. Matching sunglasses. Sharing a super burrito. Definitely yes. They wouldn't be too busy or too serious. I would remind them of a grandkid.

"Excuse me?" I said. "¿Perdón?"

They put down their forks. I smiled. They smiled back.

I turned to the man. "Well, I was only wondering, sir, would you tell me her favorite song?"

He was going to say "Volver." I knew it would be "Volver."

I was five when Dad taught us "Volver" so we could sing it at Nana and Tata's big anniversary party. By the time we were finished, everyone was crying. I mean, *everyone.* Tías, tíos, cousins, neighbors. Even the waiters who had been carrying cake to all the tables.

"You know, I think these kids have something," Dad told Mom on the drive home. He was looking at me in the rearview mirror.

The woman on the patio chuckled. She covered her mouth with a napkin.

The man looked at her and put his hand over his heart. "'Volver,'" he said.

"I think I know that one." Of course I knew that one.

Flor was back from the counter by the time I got to the final verse. I held out that last note long and sad and broken, just like we practiced with Dad. When it finally faded away, the woman lifted her sunglasses to dab her eyes with her napkin. The man tipped his head at me. The people at the next table over had stopped eating to listen too. They clapped politely. I took a step back so Flor could move in with the cup.

But she didn't move.

I nudged her with my shoulder, still grinning at the man and woman at the table. "Cup!" I whispered out of the side of my mouth.

"Oh!" She held the cup out but didn't make eye contact. We would have to work on that. Eye contact was everything. Even so, the old man stood halfway up to pull his wallet from his back pocket. He peeled off two one-dollar bills and tucked them into Flor's cup. Not a bad start.

"Thank you so much," I said. I curtsied and moved on.

Over at the counter, the manager watched us from behind the order window.

"She doesn't mind, does she?" I asked.

"As long as we don't scare anyone away, Carolina says it's all right. Here's your hot water."

Steam filled my nose as I took a careful sip. "Gah!" I burned my tongue, but I could already feel the hot, lemony water soothe my throat. Or maybe it was just the rush of a good performance. I searched the patio for our next table.

"There." I handed the water back to Flor.

This one would be risky. Definitely a tougher crowd than my first: two men, each with a glass of soda drunk down to the last drops. One stabbed a piece of lettuce—all that was left of his taco salad—with a fork. Between them, a toddler sat on a booster seat. The table in front of her was covered in rice. Chunks of refried beans clung to her hair. A bright red Icee stain dripped down the middle of her pink T-shirt.

They were tired. They were about ready to leave for the day. Plus, I didn't know what kind of mood the little girl was in, which made the whole thing even riskier. If she started crying when I started singing, they'd get up and leave in a hurry. No tip. And the manager might think we'd scared them off.

But if she liked it, and I kept her happy—well, then they might stay for a second song.

I couldn't ask for a request this time. They'd only say no, thank you, and I wasn't going to give them that chance. I marched up to the table, tickled the little girl under her arm, and said, "I bet you like to dance."

I spun around to find Flor. "Do you know 'Ay, Chabela'?"

"What, me? No!" She started to back away. She let those bangs of hers fall over her face like they were a curtain she could pull shut whenever she didn't want anyone to see her.

"All you have to do is clap," I said, as sweetly as I could. Then I mouthed impatiently, *Come on.* Her shoulders drooped, and she set the cups on the ground next to her.

"Thank you." I tapped the beat out against my hip until she got a feel for it and started to clap along.

I had only sung a little of the song when one of the men began wiping the rice off the table and crumpling their napkins and straw wrappers into one tidy pile. I thought it was over. He'd get up and throw away the trash, then they'd all leave and I'd be singing to nobody.

But then the little girl started smacking her hands against the table—right in time with Flor.

"That's right!" I shouted. I took the Cholula bottle from the middle of their table and crooned into it like a microphone. The little girl squealed and bounced on top of the booster seat.

When the man did get up, it was only to order another Fanta.

I didn't see how much money they dropped into Flor's cup after I finished the second song, but it looked like more than we got at the first table.

The plan—*my* plan—was working. It made me feel as full of bubbles as their orange soda. But it also made me overconfident. I should have noticed how lively the conversation was at the next table I stopped at. Instead, I walked right up and started my serenade. One of them rolled his eyes. "No. Please. Not now."

"Sorry!" My cheeks burned. I didn't have my own bangs to hide behind, so I pulled the brim of my hat down lower.

Flor skittered up behind me. "What now?" she whispered.

I wasn't sure. I started to bite my thumbnail but then reached for the lemon water instead. It was lukewarm and sort of bitter.

You can't make everyone like you, I reminded myself as I swallowed it anyway.

Someone interrupted my thoughts. "Excuse me? Excuse me?"

"I think they're talking to you," Flor said.

Great. Probably someone with a complaint. Someone who'd ask me to keep quiet so they could eat in peace. Well, we would just wait until they were finished and try again after they left.

I walked over, prepared to say sorry to them too. Instead, one of them asked, "Are you taking requests?"

It was a big family. They had pushed three of the patio tables together and still barely fit around them. Backpacks, jackets, and carnival prizes were piled under and behind their chairs.

"We didn't know you played here too!" a woman in a polka-dotted tank top said. "Where's the rest of the band?" She looked behind me, searching for Junior and Ronnie.

I glanced over at Flor, but she wasn't listening. She was reading the ingredients off an empty carton of Good & Plenty someone had left on the table. I realized I still hadn't told her exactly who I was. And she hadn't asked. But I was so happy someone recognized me, I didn't really stop to think about it.

"Well, it's just me this afternoon. And of course I take requests!"

"It's my tía's birthday," the woman said, wrapping her arm around another lady whose reddish-brown hair had streaks of white at the temples.

I nodded. This one would be easy. "One, two, three," I counted off before leading them through "Las Mañanitas," and after that, "Happy Birthday." It was our biggest tip that afternoon.

Flor stopped me after another two tables. "I think we have it!"

I was almost sorry we were finished.

We took the cup to an empty table and counted the money twice. With the rest of my quarters, it was enough to buy the rabbit. There was even a little left over to give Carolina.

"Thanks so much for helping us out," I said, passing her a few dollars through the window.

"Come back anytime," she said, refusing the money. "You too, Flor. I've never seen this place so busy on a Sunday afternoon. If you ever get tired of the petting zoo, you come right over here."

"I'll never get tired of the petting zoo," Flor said.

We left the Cantina a second time. It was cooler now,

getting late. The light was softer, the sun no longer blazing straight down on our heads like it had been most of the afternoon. I needed to get back to my family. Just one more stop.

At the livestock manager's office, Flor took a deep breath and said, "Let's hope this works." She took our money to the cashier. "For Number 210, please."

The cashier pulled an index card out of a container. "Edith deCarli?" She squinted down at us.

"Yes. I mean, no," Flor sputtered. "She—I mean, *Edith*—sent us to pick up one of her animals."

"The rabbit," I added.

Flor

(5:30 P.M.)

"C onejo," Randy said. "Rabbit."

"You want to name him Rabbit?" For a singer, it was not very creative.

"Well, you already have a goat named Goat. He'll fit right in, don't you think?"

"Fit in? Aren't you going to take him?"

Randy's laugh came out like a bark. "Ha! There's not enough room for us inside Wicked Wanda as it is. There's no way my dad will let me have a pet. You can keep him, can't you? Maybe your dad won't even notice one more rabbit."

"He'll notice, but he won't mind. He probably *should* mind, but he won't."

Randy stopped walking and tilted her head. "What do you mean?"

"I just mean that Papá loves taking care of animals. I'm not sure he ever meant to turn it into a business. Sometimes I don't think he knows how." Randy was quiet. I wasn't sure why I had told her that. I hadn't told anyone before. I cuddled Conejo against my cheek. "But you won't eat too much, will you?"

"Nope," Randy squeaked in what must've been her rabbit voice. "You'll hardly know I'm there."

We started walking again, and I tucked Conejo's head back under my elbow. That way, he wouldn't see anything that might startle him. Randy skipped up a few steps ahead of me to clear a path.

I wanted to tell her she could come to the petting zoo anytime to visit Conejo. She could still think of him as her pet, even though he didn't live with her. But I caught myself. If her performance didn't go well that night, if she didn't perform at all, she might not be at the carnival very much longer.

And if her performance *did* go well, there might not be a petting zoo left to visit, and I didn't know where Conejo, or any of us, would go then. The thought of it brought the sour-sick feeling back to my stomach, but not the eye-stinging anger. The Miranda I'd met at Rancho Maldonado earlier that afternoon didn't seem like the same person as the Randy who was walking back there with me. But she was. The only difference was that now she was a real person to me. A friend, maybe.

She stopped. "Oh, is that your pig? She's cute!"

"Betabel? What's she doing out? She might look cute, but don't let her fool you." I caught up and looked over at the zoo, where Papá was standing with a man wearing a gray suit coat with jeans and a straw cowboy hat. Betabel was between them, rooting around the grass, then nibbling out of the man's hand. It must have been the man from the pig farm, finally here to help us.

His timing was perfect. If he could show us how to get Betabel comfortable around people, maybe Papá could trust her with the guests. Maybe I could finally finish teaching her how to ride that skateboard, and Randy and I could both stay on at the carnival.

I lifted Conejo and whispered into his ear, "Let's sneak you in while Papá's busy talking. Then we'll find out what they're saying about Betabel."

Randy followed me around to the back of the petting zoo and into the supply shed, where Betabel liked to nap during the day. Against the wall, there was an empty hutch that we set aside for animals that needed to be kept alone because they were sick or hurt or tired. I showed Randy where to find a clean bottle of water and a dish of feed. Then I set Conejo down inside.

When Randy got back with the feed and water, she reached in and scratched his neck. Then she started humming.

"He likes that," I said.

Rabbits are nervous animals. They stress easily. But Conejo was calm considering everything he had been through that day. And he did not mind being handled. Lucinda must have done a good job raising him.

We would have to watch for a while—to make sure he wasn't a biter or a scratcher—but I had a feeling Conejo *would* fit right in at Rancho Maldonado. He would scamper through the hay and eat oatmeal out of people's hands. We'd let the littlest kids run their fingers through his fur, the same golden color as four o'clock sunshine.

"So that's your trailer?" Randy had gotten up and was standing just outside the shed. "You don't park in the lot with everyone else?"

I gave Conejo one last scratch, swung the top back over his new hutch, and fastened the latch. "There you go, little guy. Welcome home." Then I dusted off my hands and joined Randy outside.

"Papá likes us to be close to the animals to make sure none of them need anything and that no one gets in here and tries to bother them."

She unfolded one of the lawn chairs that leaned against the shed and sat.

"I've been thinking all afternoon that you looked familiar somehow, and I wondered if it was because I'd seen you in the RV lot. That's where we park Wicked Wanda. But I guess not."

"Guess not."

I was starting to think Ms. Alverson was right. I should have made friends with Randy earlier that summer. Ms. Alverson—if she had been there—she would have told me it was not too late. She would have said that right that very second would have been the perfect time to tell Randy that she didn't recognize me from the parking lot; she probably recognized me from the Family Side Stage. To tell her I had seen her show every day since she got here. To admit that I was not *just* going there for a spot to sit in the shade, but because she was a good singer and I really liked the show.

To tell her what had happened there that afternoon.

I almost said something. She seemed like the kind of person who would have wanted to help. But there was nothing she could do to help. Instead, I asked, "Want to meet Betabel?"

We cut through the hay bales that kept guests from wandering behind the pens, and back to the front of the petting zoo. Two nuns in black habits combed the sheep's wool while it stood lazily chewing on hay. Cricket nudged a man's shin with her head until he finally opened up his bag of feed again and knelt to give her what was left. The rooster crowed. Everyone froze, then everyone laughed.

Papá was still talking to the man in the gray suit coat, only now Betabel was wearing a halter. She shook her head, trying to jostle it off.

Papá clipped on a leash. The man took it. I thought,

She's already leash trained. When is he going to teach us something new?

But then he started walking away.

"What's going on?" I burst out, leaving Randy behind. "Where is he taking Betabel?"

"Flor, there you are!" Papá said. "I'm so glad you're here. I sent Mikey and Maria out to look for you—I was worried you would be too late."

"Too late?"

Papá wrung his hands. "Too late to say good-bye. I knew you would want to. This is Mr. Forrest, you know, from the pig rescue. He says there is plenty of room for Betabel at Black Walnut Hollow." He turned to the man. "Thanks again for meeting us here."

The man held out his hand to me, but I didn't take it.

Papá was sending Betabel away with a complete stranger? Sure, she was cranky and stubborn and sometimes she snapped at us, but that was not supposed to matter. We were supposed to look out for one another. We were supposed to be a family.

"No! He can't have her."

Papá tucked his hands in his pockets. He looked at Mr. Forrest. "She's eleven," he said with small shrug. I despised that.

Mr. Forrest nodded like he understood completely, and I despised that even more. "You know, I've just remembered I need to make a quick phone call," he said. "If you'll excuse me, I'll only be a moment."

Papá took the leash back, then brushed my bangs out of my eyes.

Randy just stood behind us in the pen, biting her nails and watching.

I swatted Papá's hand away. "I cannot believe you're just going to send her away. She belongs with us. She belongs here. This is her home."

Papá took off his glasses, squinted at the lenses, then wiped them with the edge of his shirttail. "We talked about this, mija."

"We never talked about this."

"I told you about the rescue farm and about Mr. Forrest coming to take a look at the pig. You thought it was a good idea."

"I thought he was coming to *help* us with her. So she wouldn't be so crabby all the time."

Papá put his glasses back on. "Pues, that is just what he came for."

"So he's not taking Betabel away?"

"No, Flor, es la razón. That's *why* he's taking Betabel away. To socialize her. She is not happy here. You've seen that. She belongs with other pigs. It would not be fair to keep her here."

I dropped to the ground, threw my arms around Betabel's neck, and cried into her bristly shoulder. She snorted and tottered away. She could not stand criers either. I scratched her back instead. Her tail swished.

"Pero, did it have to be today? Does it have to be now? I was teaching her to ride una patineta. She was making progress."

Papá smiled.

"It has to be today because this is the last night of the fair. We will be on the road again tomorrow, and we might not be in Dinuba again for another year." Then his voice got softer. "And quién sabe if the zoo will last that long. Better for Betabel to go to a good home now than for us to scramble to find someone to take her when we're desperate, ¿que no?"

So he *had* noticed what was happening to the zoo, and he was not even trying to save it.

"But I am glad you got back in time to say good-bye," Papá said. "And Mr. Forrest says we can come visit Betabel any time we're in town."

I got up, sniffed, and wiped my eyes. "No," I said. "What for? She's just a pig."

Miranda

(5:45 P.M.)

I reached my arm out and tried to stop her. "Flor?"

She snarled back, "Leave me alone."

So I did.

We watched her storm off, Mr. Maldonado and I. He shifted his weight from one foot to the other and glanced at me, like maybe I knew what she was thinking. But I didn't. I just shook my head. He shook his head too, patted the pig, and shoved his hands back in his pockets.

I'd never had a pet before, not unless you counted Conejo, and you couldn't exactly count him. But I did know what it felt like to say good-bye. To friends, to school, to home. To knowing what was going to happen next. It didn't even matter if it was all for the best. "For the best" didn't always smooth out the sharp, shattered edges of the hole that was left when you really missed something, or when you were afraid that nothing would turn out the way you hoped it would.

Dad meant it when he promised us that all his plans and all his decisions were for the best. But he didn't know for sure. None of us did. Every Monday morning, while we waited in the motor home for the carnival to pack up and get ready to move on, I put on my headphones and pretended to listen to my Spanish lessons. But really I was worrying about whether the people in the next town would like us, whether they would like *me*.

Flor had said she wanted to be left alone, but I wondered if she really meant it. No matter how frustrated I was with Dad's plans and how there was never any room to stretch outside the margins of his notebook, no matter how nervous I was that I'd never sing and dance on the big stages of my dreams, I always felt better knowing I could count on Ronnie and Junior to be there with me.

I knew they were counting on me too and that I should get back to them, but I wanted to wait a little longer for Flor. I wanted to thank her for changing her mind and showing me around the carnival all afternoon. I wanted to tell her I was sorry about her pig, and if she felt like it, that she should come see our show.

And cold hard fact: I also wanted to see if she was mad

at me. She had seemed kind of mad at me when she rushed away, and maybe she had a good reason. If I hadn't insisted on singing at Carolina's Cantina, maybe we would've gotten back to Rancho Maldonado in time for her to stop her dad from giving away the pig.

But if it hadn't been for Carolina's Cantina, we wouldn't have been able to rescue Conejo, and no one could be angry about that, could they?

Flor

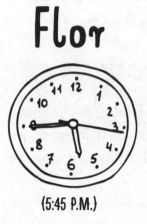

(5:45 P.M.)

The wheels of Betabel's old skateboard rolled *ba-bump*, *ba-bump* over the pebbly dirt floor of the shed. I just sat there pushing it back and forth, back and forth.

It was a dumb idea. I saw that now. The thing of it was, I had really and truly thought it might work.

I got up and stomped my foot when I thought about how proud I had been when I finally coaxed Betabel onto the skateboard, and about the loose change I had been saving up to buy her a new one.

I stomped my foot because Papá knew all along the zoo was in trouble, and that meant things must have been even worse than I'd realized.

I stomped my foot because I couldn't make myself stop crying.

It was not the first time I ever had to say good-bye to an animal. Animals were born and animals died. Animals came and went. Bringing them home meant letting them go someday. Always.

But this was different. It was more than saying good-bye to Betabel. It was saying good-bye to the idea that all of this—the petting zoo and the carnival—could stay the same forever. That I would never have to leave the place where I finally had friends, knew all the rules, and wasn't the only one who was a little bit strange.

But Betabel was going—Betabel was probably gone—and it seemed like no matter how hard I tried, I would have to go too. I sat back down, hugged my knees, and picked at a thin spot in my blue jeans. Any day now, it would rip. The thing of it was, no one would even notice at the carnival. But they would at school. Someone always noticed your mistakes, your bad luck, the patches your mamá sewed over the holes in your jeans. It was why I didn't want to go back.

I blinked hard when my eyes went all blurry again. When I opened them, I noticed something up on the counter. Betabel's kettle corn was right where I had left it earlier that afternoon. I jumped up and grabbed the bag. There was still a little left inside. Betabel would want it. Betabel would need it.

There was no way that man, Mr. Forrest, would know it was her favorite. How could he?

I had to stop him before he took her away without it.

Racing back to the front of the zoo, I nearly tripped over the skateboard. I kicked it out of the way, and it rolled straight into the metal wall of the shed, knocking over the currycombs and nail clippers that had been resting on a shelf. They clattered to the ground. But I couldn't stop to pick up the mess. I still had a chance to catch up and say good-bye to Betabel like the friend she was.

Then that chance slipped away too.

By the time I made it up front, all I saw was Papá, his hands back in his pockets, watching Betabel and Mr. Forrest get smaller and smaller as he led her by the leash toward the exit. Eventually, I lost them in the crowd. I would never find them.

"Flor?"

Randy was in the corner of the pen with Chivo on her lap. She set him down and stood. She was probably trying to be nice. She probably wanted to help. But she didn't realize that the only way she could help me now was if she didn't sing.

Her sister and brother—the girl with the accordion, the boy with the guitar—were probably waiting for her. It must have been time to get dressed or warm up or whatever it is people do when the spotlight is about to shine on them.

If I wanted to stop her, it had to be now. This was my last chance.

But it was only a thread of a chance, thin and frayed and about to snap.

Anyway, I had already tried everything. There was nothing in a carnival food stand so spicy, sweet, or sour it could unsettle her stomach. And there wasn't any ride that spun fast enough to knock her off balance. So I decided Mr. Reyes must have been right. Miranda was main-stage material, and I couldn't stop her.

I would tell her good luck and to leave me alone.

Then, like the sparkle of one more last chance, the lights of the midway rides blinked on.

Mr. Barsetti had them on a timer. It was a waste of electricity, he said, to keep the lights on while the sun was still shining so bright. So it wasn't until closer to sunset that the midway lit up. The Ferris wheel blinked pink and gold. Blue chevrons flashed along the sides of the Zipper as it tumbled end over end. The carousel horses pranced under a pearly glow. You could hear everyone say "Aaaah."

And all around the top of the Cloud Chaser, lights twinkled purple, orange, yellow, green.

It was a high-flying swing ride and one of our oldest. It broke down more than it should have, at least once a weekend. Passengers dangled over the midway like stuffed animals over a carnival game booth until the mechanic arrived to get the ride moving again. They usually weren't stranded for more than fifteen minutes or so. But sometimes it took longer to get everyone down. Sometimes a lot longer.

I could ask Miranda Reyes for one ride on the Cloud Chaser, and maybe it would run perfectly smoothly. We would get on, we would get off, and I would know I had tried everything I could to save the zoo. She had a future on the main stage, and there was just no keeping her from it.

Or we'd get stuck up there.

"Are you all right?" Randy asked. She looked worried. She looked like she cared. I swallowed hard.

Miranda

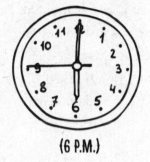

(6 P.M.)

She didn't answer me right away, so I asked again.

"Are you all right?"

Flor had come running out to the front of Rancho Maldonado just as I was about to get up to go look for her.

Her eyes were red and her cheeks were all splotchy. She sniffled and wiped her nose with the back of her hand. For a second I thought she might run away again, back to the shed or after her pig. But she was still, staring at the carnival rides behind me.

She batted her hair out of her face. "Have you ever been on the Cloud Chaser?"

I knew I should have been rehearsing. Dad was probably pacing inside Wicked Wanda, wondering where I was. Actually, he was probably stomping back and forth *in front* of Wanda, gnawing on that pencil he always kept in his shirt pocket to make notes on our performances. There wasn't enough room inside for the kind of pacing he'd be doing this close to showtime.

At least the line wasn't very long. If I got back by 6:15, we would still have an hour to practice and check the sound. That would leave me with only ten minutes or so for hair and makeup, but since Dad had banned makeup and I'd be wearing a hat, it probably wouldn't take that long anyway.

I wiped my palms on the sides of my skirt. As bad as I felt about disappointing Dad, I felt worse about letting Ronnie and Junior down. I could tell them I'd gotten lost on the fairgrounds, or that I had gotten stuck in the crowd. Or I could tell them the truth: that Flor had said a ride would help cheer her up, and I just couldn't say no.

I stood on tiptoe to see how many people were still ahead of us.

"Do you have somewhere to be, or something?" Flor asked.

Maybe she was still angry. Maybe she thought I wanted to back out.

"Yes. But, no. I mean, I *do* have somewhere to be, but not right this second. I have some time. It's just that my dad's been expecting me. For hours. That's all."

The line lurched forward.

"If you don't want to be here..."

"No, I do."

The Cloud Chaser was round like a carousel, only instead of horses it had swings that hung from the top by metal chains. And instead of turning in slow circles to an old Wurlitzer recording, it rose above the rooftops and turned so fast the swings flew out slantways.

Don't scream, I reminded myself. There wouldn't be enough lemon wedges on the whole fairgrounds to save my voice after what I'd already put it through that day.

Another group of riders raced out to find their seats. "Fasten your seat belts," the operator said. Everyone fastened their seat belts. Everyone followed directions. I was good at it too, following directions. I pulled down on the brim of my ball cap.

Maybe the only reason I had made it this far was because I had always done whatever Dad told me to. Maybe if I stopped listening to him, I would never make it any further.

Cold, hard fact: I might never have even found those nachos if Flor hadn't been there to tell me where to go.

I had thought I was taking charge when she and I went back to Carolina's Cantina to sing for tips, but even then,

138

I was still just following Dad's plan. Step by step, the same routine we had followed every weekend before we joined the carnival.

Flor hadn't taken her eyes off the ride for more than a moment or two since we got in line. She watched it climb, turn, come down again.

I tried to get her attention. "Hey."

She just kept staring.

"Hey," I said again, louder.

She faced me. "We don't have to get on if you don't want to."

"What? No, that's not what I meant. It's just, can I ask you a question?"

"Yeah?"

"When we were talking about the side stage earlier? And you said you heard the band was overrated? Well, what exactly have you heard about them?"

I held my hands behind my back to keep from biting my nails.

Flor turned toward the Cloud Chaser again. She tucked her bangs behind her ears.

"Oh, the *side-stage* band? I thought we were talking about some other band. I heard the side-stage act is pretty good, actually. Great lead singer."

I knew she was only saying what she'd *heard*, but still, I was almost as thrilled and surprised as when Dad had told us we'd be playing on the main stage. I wanted to ask more, but it was our turn to get on. The guy taking tickets held up his hand for a high five. Flor met it limply. "You're new around here, aren't you?" he said, waving me through. "Good thing you have Flor to show you what's what."

Floor tilted her neck and looked up at the ride. "How's she running today?"

The guy looked up too. "So far, so good," he said, knocking on a wooden fence post. "No problems all weekend."

Flor

(6:05 P.M.)

We buckled into two metal swings. Randy sat on the outside edge, and I chose the spot right next to her. Metal chains creaked and clanged as other passengers barreled around the ride to claim their seats. Just in front of us, a mom lifted her small daughter into a chair and tightened the safety belt before sitting down too.

"Don't look so nervous," she said, reaching over and tousling the girl's hair. "This was my favorite when I was your age. You are going to love it."

Our shadows stretched long onto the patchy brown grass. The heat had broken, but the fairgrounds still felt warm and sunbaked. It was the best part of the day, or would have been if that knot in my stomach hadn't been so twisted up and tangled.

Randy kicked her legs forward and pulled them back. Kicked forward, pulled back. Her chair swung lazily as we waited for all the seats to fill. She glanced over her shoulder as if she were looking for someone. The little girl in front of us clung tightly to the chains on either side of her swing. "Relax," her mom said. "You'll be fine."

It was the kind of thing parents said a little too easily, if you asked me. They wanted you to be fine. They thought you probably would be in the end. But all you could do was hang on tight until you knew for sure.

"Please buckle your seat belts and remain seated until the ride has come to a full and complete stop."

The swings jerked upward a few inches, and the little girl yelped.

"Whoa!" Randy said, giggling. She pulled her hat off and held it in her lap, then shook her hair out and leaned backward in the swing.

The soles of my shoes just skimmed the ground. Then only the very tips of my toes were touching, and the space between the ground and me kept growing.

The ride had been running well, Dave had said. No problems all weekend. Everything would probably be fine. The Cloud Chaser would rotate, just like it was supposed to. Two or three minutes later—too soon for some riders—it would slow, then stop, then bring us back down. Then, just like she was supposed to, Miranda would find her way to the main stage, look out at the audience, tip her cowboy hat, tap her boots, and sing.

The tower at the center of the ride stretched taller, hoisted us higher, and finally began to turn, flinging our swings outward like the edges of a twirling dance skirt.

Still leaning back in her chair, Randy closed her eyes and threw her arms out on either side of her. She looked like a kite that had escaped its string.

I held on. The breeze whisked the hair out of my eyes. From above, the whole fair—from the golden top of the carousel to the red-striped tents of the midway games, all lined up like peppermint sticks—looked small enough to bundle up and hold in my arms. Someone near the Cantaloupe Growers Association demonstration garden let go of a pink helium balloon. I watched it float over the Log Jammer and above the telephone wires until I lost track of it in the evening sky, the same milky orange as a Creamsicle.

The girl in front of us leaned forward and peered over the edge of her seat. She loosened her grip on the chains and uncurled her fingers one at a time until she wasn't holding on at all anymore. She lifted her hands up over her head for one daring moment. Then she pulled them right back in again.

I closed one eye and held out my finger to trace the map of every place I had been that long afternoon. From Rancho Maldonado—near the entrance, by the ticket booths—to the

Family Side Stage right in the middle. Folding chairs under a white sailcloth tent.

From the midway, where softballs were still knocking down milk bottles and squirt guns were still missing their targets, to the Gravitron, to the churro cart, to the livestock barns way out at the muddy edges of the fairgrounds. The auctions were over. The stalls would be empty by now. The kids would have cleaned them and gone home with their ribbons, or just their broken hearts.

Under the lights of the Cloud Chaser, I knew exactly where I was.

I looked farther, past the exit, past the parking lots, where people did not always look out for one another, and guardrails did not always keep you from getting hurt. I didn't want to have to find my way through that world again. In that world, I was as lost as a stray balloon. But every turn of the Cloud Chaser brought me closer to it.

After a few minutes, before I was ready, the ride slowed and stopped. The chains on the swings hung straight and still.

"What's happening?" the little girl in front of us asked her mom.

"That's it," the mom said. "The ride is over, that's all. We'll have to get off now. Didn't you like it, though? Didn't we have fun?"

The Cloud Chaser began to lower us back to the ground.

But then something deep inside it grumbled and groaned, and the ride didn't budge another inch.

Miranda

(6:15 P.M.)

I could feel the Cloud Chaser slow down and start to drop. But I was surprised when it suddenly stopped moving altogether. I wiggled my feet and stretched my toes downward, but they still didn't touch the ground. I opened my eyes, then sat up. We were still high in the air, just dangling.

I turned to Flor. "What's going on?"

She craned her neck over the edge of her seat. "I don't know. Something must have happened to the ride. Sometimes...it... stalls." Her eyes darted across the ground below.

"It *stalls*?"

"Dave!" she shouted at the ground. "Dave!"

The guy who had let us on peeked out from inside the

operating booth. He held one hand up to shield his eyes and waved to Flor with the other one.

"Everything's okay!" he yelled. "Don't worry! We'll have you back down here before you know it."

Flor covered her face with her hands. "Nooooo," she moaned.

"It stalls?"

Flor lifted her hands. "Sometimes?"

The little girl sitting in front of us whimpered. I wanted to cry too.

While we were still soaring over the midway, I had closed my eyes to try to imagine that night's performance—like I always did when I was nervous before a show. I pictured us onstage in our matching cowboy hats, the audience cheering, the silver studs on our vests glinting under the spotlight. I thought about Ronnie tapping out the beat before she and Junior started playing, how I could feel it even though I couldn't always hear it. And I thought about the beat that fell right before it was time for me to sing, the one that felt like the last, no-turning-back breath you take before diving into a swimming pool, the one that fills your lungs with daring.

I imagined dancing across the stage and holding my microphone out for the audience to sing along to all those old songs they knew by heart.

I imagined Junior, head bent to his guitar strings, trying to stay on pace, but also wanting to break free and race faster and faster. I knew how that felt too, holding yourself back when you wished you could leap ahead.

I was ready. Still, I couldn't ignore the nagging worry that Dad's plan was wrong this time and I needed to show the audience who I really was, and not just who he thought I should be.

The girl in front of us was crying even harder. Her mom was saying, "Shhh, shhh, it's all right. Shhh," trying to calm her down.

Flor swung herself forward and caught the back of the little girl's seat. "Hey," she said. "What's your name?"

The girl sniffled but didn't speak. "Go ahead," her mom said. "Tell her your name."

The girl shook her head furiously.

"That's okay," Flor said. "I only wanted to tell you that I have been on this ride hundreds of times, and I promise, Dave will bring us right back down."

"Are you sure?" I asked, even though I knew she wasn't talking to me.

"I promise," she said again to both of us. "Right back down."

"See?" the girl's mom said. "I bet it will only be a minute."

The girl gulped and stopped crying. She didn't seem convinced, though, and neither did anyone else. Below, most of the people who had been waiting to ride the Cloud Chaser had abandoned the line. The ones who stayed looked like they were only sticking around to see what would happen to us.

At the main stage, floodlights shone over the grandstand seats. The marquee flashed the name of that night's headliner. It flashed again: WITH OPENING ACT MIRANDA Y LOS REYES.

The audience would've begun lining up by now. Dad would have to tell Mr. Barsetti I was missing. He would ask him to wait just a little while longer. "She'll be here."

Dave popped out of the booth again, this time with a megaphone. "We apologize for the delay. Please remain seated."

Permanezcan sentados, I thought.

"What else are we going to do?" someone shouted. Riders muttered and twisted in their swings.

"Get us down from here!"

"What's going on?"

The little girl sobbed.

"Don't worry," Flor said. "I know that guy, and he's going to fix the ride, okay?" She tapped her finger against her lips. "Ummm...Hey, do you have a favorite animal?"

"You like cats," the girl's mom prompted.

"You like cats? *I* like cats!" I wasn't there to critique her performance, but Flor sounded just a teensy bit too excited for a conversation about cats. On the other hand, the girl had switched from crying to chewing on the inside of her cheek.

"When I was little like you, I used to live on a farm. And at the farm, we had a cat. It was an outside cat, though. A mouser. Not really a pet."

I started humming. Then singing. Couldn't stop myself.

"And on that farm they had a cat."

The girl turned around. The very edges of her lips curled upward. *"E-I-E-I-O,"* she sang back.

"What?" Flor scrunched up her nose. She was still talking about all the rats that old farm cat used to eat.

"Oh, you're going to have to be louder than that," I told the girl. "Try again. One, two... *Maldonado had a farm.*"

The girl and her mother sang together. *"E-I-E-I-O!"*

Flor stared at me, blinking.

Come on, I mouthed at her. *"And on that farm, they had a..."*

I pointed to the girl.

"Umm...a rabbit!"

"A rabbit!" I sang. "Do you know what? I have a rabbit. His name is Rabbit."

"What do rabbits even say?" Flor protested. We ignored her. *"E-I-E-I-O!"*

"Randy, people are starting to look at you."

They weren't just looking, they were also starting to sing. *"With a hip hop here and a hip hop there."*

Flor pulled on the ends of her hair. "It doesn't even make sense. That's not what rabbits *say*. That's what rabbits *do*."

"E-I-E-I-O!" I sang even louder.

The little girl was laughing now. "Again!"

I swung over to Flor to give her my hat so I could clap along. "Hold this!"

"*And on that farm she had…*"

"A dog!" someone on the other side of the ride called out.

"Did you know that in Spanish, dogs say *guau guau* instead of *ruff ruff*?" I asked the girl.

She giggled. "*E-I-E-I-O!*"

We did chicken next, then pig, and by the time we got to donkey, everyone was singing. Even Flor. I stopped to listen and they kept going without me. At the end of every verse, someone would shout out another animal name. And when there weren't any more animals left on the farm, they moved on to the jungle: monkey, elephant, snake.

I closed my eyes and leaned way back in my chair. I stretched out my arms. It was silly and strange, but I felt like I was floating again. Like a kite chasing clouds in clear-blue sky, but also like the breeze that was lifting it up.

Just as someone called out, "Sea lion!" the ride rattled and wheezed back to life. It lowered us gently to the ground, and when our feet finally touched concrete, everyone cheered.

I unlatched my safety belt and jumped from the swing to take a bow. The cheers were even louder.

I knew why I couldn't ignore my doubts about Dad's plan. I didn't need him to tell me exactly what to sing and exactly how to sing it anymore, and unless I started doing things my way, it wouldn't really be me up there. I'd never really *connect*. It'd just be Dad's voice, Dad's dream.

But he wasn't going to listen unless I made him. He

wouldn't take me seriously unless I didn't play. It would mean betraying Junior and Ronnie. The thought made my chest feel like rubber bands were squeezing my heart. Still, there wasn't any other way.

The little girl's mom squeezed my hand and thanked me for distracting her daughter until the ride got fixed. A few other people clapped my back and told me, "Nice job."

"Can I talk you into riding this contraption full-time?" Dave joked. "It breaks down at least once a weekend. This is the first time no one's demanded a refund."

"*Once a weekend?* You could have warned me!"

Flor grimaced.

"Well, I don't know about full-time," I said. "But I'd take another turn if that's okay?"

"You're not afraid of getting stuck again?" he asked.

"Nope."

"Well, then, be my guest." He held out his arm, but Flor stood in my way.

"We can't," she said.

"We can—he just said we could."

"No. You have to get back. You said your dad has been expecting you."

"Not anymore," I said. "I changed my mind. Let's go!" I tried to push past her.

She stepped in front of me again. "No, you have to go. You're going to be late. Hurry up."

Flor

(6:30 P.M.)

I should have been happy or at least relieved. I should have been searching for Mikey and his giant pink gorilla to tell him it had taken me all afternoon, but I had done it. I had gotten exactly what I wanted. Even better than what I wanted. I hadn't had to make her sick or strain her voice or strand her on a ride—not for very long, anyway. Randy had decided on her own not to sing that night.

The thing of it was, she had finally decided it right when I realized she *had* to sing.

I looked over my shoulder. Randy had fallen behind, watching some girl sink basket after basket at the Hoop Shoot.

"No, no, no." I ground my teeth and marched back over to her. "Randy, let's go. We have to get you back."

"You have to see this—she's up to twelve in a row!" She did not even look at me. "Oh! This isn't another trick, is it? Is there a secret to winning?"

The girl tucked the basketball under her arm and glowered at us.

"No, it isn't a trick. But you cannot stay here. Your dad is expecting you." I took hold of her wrist and pulled.

"Hey!"

There was only an hour before the show. It would be far too late for Mr. Barsetti to find another replacement band. If Randy didn't get there, the concert would have to go on without an opening act. After a slipup like that, the Reyes family would be lucky to keep their spot on the carnival, let alone steal ours.

But that was not the only reason I had to fix this, or even the most important. Mr. Reyes had been right. Randy did not belong on the side stage. She was main-stage material, even when she wasn't onstage. Up there on the Cloud Chaser, she had soaked up all our restlessness and worry and turned it into a song. And she loved doing it as much as I loved taking care of our animals. Miranda had earned her big chance, and I was the one stealing it from *her*.

"I told you, I'm not going back. It's the only way to make my dad listen."

"But you have to."

A couple strolled ahead of us holding hands. I tore between them. We did not have time to slow down even a little. I was trying to decide whether we would get to their motor home faster if we cut through the exhibition halls or if we kept on tromping down the midway, when someone called her name.

"Miranda!"

Then mine.

"Flor!" It was Ms. Alverson, leaning as far out of that giant lemon as she could without falling through the window.

"Miranda! Your brother and your sister have been looking everywhere for you. Your parents are about to call security. They said to send you straight on over to the arena."

Ms. Alverson must have known Randy better than I realized she did.

"Flor, you can get her there in a hurry, can't you? I'm glad you finally made friends, but I didn't mean for you to make her miss her big break."

"Finally?" Randy asked.

"Sure, she's been watching your show all summer. I kept telling her the two of you would get along. I'm glad she finally listened. Now, scoot!"

"You watch my show?"

I did not answer. I was already on my way. "Come on!" The arena wasn't far. It was closer than the parking lot, right by the first aid tent. We were not too late. We would make it. I was not going to let Miranda lose her chance, even if it meant losing mine. We were all family and we looked out for one another.

She was still galloping after me, telling me to slow down and wait a minute.

Finally, she shouted, "*STOP!*" It was like I said, she was small, but she had a voice like fireworks bursting. Only this time, it was more like a bundle of dynamite.

So I stopped.

She just stood there staring at me like she was trying to figure something out. She didn't say anything for a long moment, so I kept on walking. "You are going to be late. We should get going. We're almost there."

"You've seen our show? You knew who I was? All along?"

I stopped again. "I knew who you were, but I didn't really *know* you. If I had known, I would have—"

She was still staring, but with her black eyebrows all wrinkled. I couldn't blame her. It didn't make sense to me either.

I nodded. "I knew."

"Well then, how come you pretended you didn't? I don't understand."

A whole circus parade of excuses and explanations marched across my mind:

I didn't know for sure who she was.

I thought she'd want her privacy.

I wasn't allowed to go to the Family Side Stage, and if anyone found out, there'd be trouble.

None of them were very good. Any of them would have meant more questions, and more questions meant more time, which we did not have. So I took a deep breath and told her the truth.

"I never miss the noon show at the Family Side Stage. I've been going since before you even got here. And today, when I was there, I heard your dad talking to Mr. Barsetti, telling him you were main-stage material and why doesn't he give you a chance."

"So?"

"So then your dad said if you were a main-stage act, you deserved higher pay. But the only way Mr. Barsetti can afford to pay you any more is if he cuts another act. Like us. Like the petting zoo. *Your dad* said Mr. Barsetti should kick us off the carnival. So I had to stop you from singing."

She hugged her stomach, curling into herself like I had just socked her in the gut.

Then she straightened. "I knew I recognized you," she said, pointing at my chest. "I recognized you from the very beginning. It was you. You were the one who ran out of our show before we were finished playing."

"It was me."

She almost smiled, but instead, her mouth twisted into a frown.

"So all along, you were just trying to keep me from sing-ing. This whole day? It was all some kind of trick?"

When she put it that way, it sounded terrible. I couldn't believe I had done it. I would be angry too. As angry as I had been at her that morning, only *I* knew exactly what I was doing when I was ruining her dreams.

"I am so sorry. I know I shouldn't have. That's why I'm try-ing to get you back. You deserve to be up there. I should have told you. I was just so afraid of losing the zoo and losing the animals. About going back to school and leaving this place."

"Because you're all family at Barsetti and Son?"

"That's right."

"Well, you know what? You *are* just like family. Just like my dad. Just one more person trying to control everything I do. You should've told me what was going on."

"What could you have done about it?" I snapped. "Would you have told them you wouldn't sing? Would you have stayed on the side stage so I could stay at the zoo? So I could stay at my *home*?"

She was quiet. "I don't know what I would have done. But I would have tried to help. I thought we were friends." She turned around then. "I'll get back on my own," she said as she walked away.

I was still holding her baseball cap.

Miranda

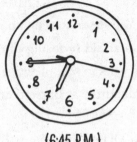

(6:45 P.M.)

All the tables at Carolina's Cantina were full again. It didn't really matter. I didn't have any money left to order food, and I didn't feel like eating. The Cantina was just the only place on the fairgrounds I knew I could find on my own. The only place besides the petting zoo, that is, and I definitely didn't want to go back there.

I thought about going back to my family, but I wasn't ready to see them yet.

But I guess it wasn't up to me.

"Randy! Hey, Randy!" Ronnie and Junior were in front of the deep-fried Twinkie booth and coming my way. I wished I had a giant pink gorilla to hide behind. I tried to cover my face, but it was too late. All I could do was wait for them to pelt me with their frustration and disappointment. I knew I deserved it.

Instead, Ronnie ran toward me, grabbed my arm, and pulled me into an enormous hug. "Oh my gosh, Randy, I thought you got lost or ran away or something."

"You're so dramatic."

"And you're so annoying," she said, thumping me on the back of the head. "We were worried. Where have you been all this time?"

"Out here, on the midway. With Flor. She's with the petting zoo, and she's my friend. Well, I thought she was my friend, but—"

Junior's eyes dropped to the ground. Ronnie's fell on her watch.

"Sorry, Randy, but we don't have time for this," she said, bunching up her eyebrows and sounding almost exactly like Dad. But unlike Junior earlier that afternoon, she wasn't kidding around. Just what I needed. Someone else telling me what to do. "We have to go. Right now. We told Dad we'd bring you straight back as soon as we found you. We still need to do a sound check, you know? We still have to get dressed. No one's been able to do anything because we've all been too busy trying to find you."

I couldn't stand the idea of everyone waiting around for me. Everyone angry and on edge, but I wasn't ready to go back. I wasn't sure I wanted to sing.

"Not yet. Just a few more minutes. Junior, please?" Junior always found his own rhythm. He sped up or he slowed down. Not like rule-following Ronnie, who wanted every beat to be sure and steady. "I just need a little—"

This time, he took her side. "Ronnie's right. It's time to go back." He rested his hand on my shoulder. "We can still run through the set if we hurry. Listen, Dad isn't mad, if that's what you're worried about. He even said sorry for putting so much pressure on us."

I shrugged out of Junior's grasp.

"I'll come back," I told Junior. "But first I just need a minute to—"

"No!" Ronnie interrupted.

My ears felt hot. I was getting sick of the two of them never letting me finish a sentence.

"Not in a minute, Miranda," she went on. "Right now. It's late. Don't you know what tonight means for you? For all of us? Don't you have any idea how important this is?"

My heart thumped faster than Junior's bass line.

"Of course I know how important this is! I gave up my room for this! I gave up my friends for this!" I could hear my voice shaking, but I kept going. "I spend all week working on my singing and worrying about my singing, and practicing my Spanish so I can be a better singer. And *then* I spend all weekend up there in front of strangers, smiling so hard it makes my cheeks sore, so you and Junior can hide behind me and never listen to what I think!"

I was out of breath. That wasn't fair and part of me wished I could snatch the words back. I knew my brother and sister worked as hard as I did. But I always thought they cared about what I had to say. Now they didn't even care enough to hear it.

Ronnie opened her mouth. Her lip quivered. But whatever it was she was about to tell me, she swallowed it back down.

Junior tossed his arms in the air. "Are you serious? We left our friends too. We miss our home too. We're not *hiding* behind you, we're pushing you forward. Toward this! To a chance like we have tonight, and you're going to blow it. You're going to throw away our whole plan."

It was a good plan. It had taken us from our garage to the church variety show, to the baseball field, to the side stage, and maybe even further. Only, it was Dad's plan, and as good as it was, it left some things out. Important things like getting so dizzy your legs turned to mush or learning the secret to winning on the midway. And trusting yourself to know what to do, even if it meant folding up your plan and sticking it back in your pocket for a while.

Ronnie used to keep a picture on her desk, over at our old house. It was of her softball team when she was in fifth grade, the last season she played. It was the same year, not long after Nana and Tata's anniversary party, that Dad strapped an accordion over her shoulders and bought Junior a hand-me-down bass guitar from one of his old band buddies. The same year we started staying up late for music lessons after they finished their homework. I was still in kindergarten. I didn't have any homework yet.

Ronnie's team made it to the semifinals that spring, but their big game was scheduled for the same weekend as this talent competition up in Kingsburg that Dad had entered.

Ronnie said she wouldn't play in the talent show.

Her team needed her, she said. She was the shortstop.

Dad tried to persuade her. He said there'd be other games, that we needed to practice playing in front of an audience. The show could be our first big break.

He promised her new cleats and a new glove if she performed.

He threatened to take away her old ones if she didn't.

Then he said we were going and that was that.

She told him he could make her go, but he couldn't make her play.

And I guess he finally believed her, because we never did go to Kingsburg.

"Ronnie?" I waited until she was looking me in the eye. "I know how important the show is. I don't want to let you down. Please. Give me five minutes." I would go back. But I wanted Dad to know it was because I decided to, not because he said so and not because Ronnie and Junior had dragged me.

Ronnie's arms hung at her sides. She squeezed her eyes shut, then opened them. "Fine," she said, so quietly I almost wasn't sure I'd really heard it.

"But Dad said—"

"It's fine," Ronnie said again, interrupting Junior but looking at me. "You'll come straight back to the arena?" She took off her watch and fastened it around my wrist. "Five minutes?"

"I promise. Five minutes," I told her. "Cinco minutos."

Flor

(6:45 P.M.)

Without thinking about where I was going, I wandered slowly back toward Rancho Maldonado. Ms. Alverson saw me and told the customer at her window, "Hang on a minute."

She poked her head out. "Did you get her back in time? How come you didn't stay to watch the show?"

I turned, and when she saw my face, she said, "Flor, you wait right there. Lexanne!"

As soon as Lexanne took over at the cash register, Ms. Alverson dashed out of the stand holding another cup of frozen lemonade. Her cure for everything. This one had a cherry on top. She must have known it was serious.

She put a hand on my cheek. It was cold and wet from the lemonade. "What happened? What's wrong? Here. Have a sip."

She held out the cup, but Papá had walked up behind me, and he was the one who took it from her.

"Thank you, Maggie," he said, "for always looking out for Flor." He put his arm around my shoulders. "Let's go, mija. It's time for dinner."

We could have eaten dinner in the cafeteria tent like most of the other people who lived and worked at the carnival. Or I could have survived just fine on snacks from the Food Pavilion. But from the first day we arrived, Mamá insisted that we eat our dinners together as a family. "If this is our home, we're going to treat it like one," she had said.

Papá would close the zoo for an hour, and we would take turns cooking—outside on the camp stove, if the weather was good, and inside the RV if it was not.

Papá and I tried to stick with the routine after Mamá left, but it was hard. We would lose track of time and it would be too late to cook, and after the groceries Mamá left us ran out, we kept forgetting to go out shopping for more.

So I was not sure what Papá had in mind when he said it was time for dinner. All I'd found in the cupboards when I made us breakfast that morning was a half-empty bag of masa harina, a box of spaghetti noodles, a bottle of Tajín, a can of corn, a can of black beans, half a lemon, and two cantaloupes from the fair.

I had decided to dice one of the cantaloupes and sprinkle Tajín on top.

Papá could not have prepared much of a dinner with what was left. But I wasn't hungry anyway.

We walked behind the petting zoo where the camp chairs were already set up on either side of an upturned crate that Papá had covered with one of our towels. "Siéntate."

While I sat down, he went to the RV and came back carrying two plates. Lined up on each one were three small tacos topped with corn-and-black-bean salsa.

"Where did all this come from?"

"From the kitchen. Pues, the turkey came from the Drumstick Wagon—I pulled the meat off the bone—but we had everything else in the kitchen."

"Not tortillas," I said.

"Masa y agua."

"But the salsa?"

"Corn and beans, plus some lemon and Tajín. I told you, we had all the ingredients."

Even though I thought I wasn't hungry, I took a bite. Mamá would have approved. No matter how good fair food tasted, it did not taste homemade.

Papá sat and folded one of his tacos in his hand. As he lifted it to his mouth, I asked, "Are we going to have to leave the carnival?"

"Pues..."

"Well, *what*? Why aren't you trying harder? Why aren't you trying at all?"

He put the taco down. "Maybe I'm not a very good businessman, and I'm sorry for that. But I *am* trying, mija. Your mamá is too."

"She isn't trying. She left. She gave up."

Papá shook his head. "We are both trying to do the best with what we have, like always. Pero if keeping the zoo open means we can't treat people, or the animals, fairly? If it means holding you back? Then it is time to leave. But wherever we go, we have what we need. We have more than you think."

I understood what he meant about being kind. Rancho Maldonado wouldn't be the same if Papá didn't have a generous heart, as frustrating as it was sometimes. But I still thought everything we needed was here. At the carnival.

Miranda

(6:55 P.M.)

Dad and Mr. Barsetti were both outside leaning against the wall when an usher led me to the entrance of our dressing room at the main-stage theater. I still wasn't in the mood to sing or to dance. Not even to smile. But I knew I had to keep my promise to Ronnie.

"I was beginning to think you had a case of stage fright, young lady," Mr. Barsetti said.

Dad unfolded his arms and whipped off his hat. "And I told you Miranda never gets stage fright. I knew she'd be here. She's main-stage material."

Dad set his hands on my shoulders and leaned down until

we were almost nose-to-nose. His eyebrows were storm clouds, and I braced myself for a torrent. But what fell was less than a drizzle. His hands slid off my shoulders. "Go inside. Get ready."

The dressing room—at least the one the opening act was assigned—was not much bigger than the inside of Wicked Wanda. It had a green vinyl chair where you could sit and put on makeup, and a mirror with little white lights all around it. Two of the bulbs were burned out, though. It had its own bathroom and a garment rack just for our costumes. Mine was the only one still hanging, ironed smooth and freshly BeDazzled. I took the vest off the hanger. "You added some rhinestones."

Mom had been sitting on a scarred leather sofa, sewing a new button onto Junior's shirt. She dropped it when she heard me, hurdled over our boots, and wrapped her arms around my neck. "You're here! You're all right." She kissed both of my cheeks, then stepped back to look at me. "Mija, you don't have to go out there if you don't want to. You don't have to do this."

The problem was, I didn't know anymore what I wanted to do or didn't want to do. I wriggled away from Mom. "I'm going to go wash my face."

I bumped into Junior on the way to the bathroom. He rubbed his knuckles on my head. "Glad you made it, sis."

"Thanks," I mumbled. I stepped around him into the bathroom and turned on the faucet. It wasn't until I looked at myself in the mirror and saw my hair, plastered to my forehead on top and snarled around my shoulders at the bottom, that I remembered Flor still had my hat.

"Figures." The hat used to remind me of how far we'd come. But maybe I hadn't made it very far after all, and maybe I wouldn't make it any further, at least without my dad and his plan.

I cupped my hands and let them fill up with water. Then I splashed it all over my face.

Ronnie knocked.

"Come out, okay? We need to get you ready."

Her makeup bag was unzipped on the countertop in front of the vanity mirror. She patted the green vinyl chair. "Sit down."

"But Dad said—"

"Don't worry about Dad. He wants people to be able to see you up there. Close your eyes." While she dusted blue eye shadow across my lids, Mom picked up the comb and started detangling my hair, humming a song—"*El Rey*," I thought— while she worked through the knots. Junior was on the couch with his guitar, warming up his fingers.

Dad came in just as Ronnie was dabbing peachy-pink gloss on my lips. When our eyes met in the mirror, I thought he'd tell me to go back to the bathroom and wash it all off again, but he just handed me a paper cup of tea.

I sniffed. No lemon.

Dad backed away and sat next to Junior on the couch. He cleared his throat. "Escuchen."

Junior put down his guitar, and Ronnie snapped her makeup compact shut. Mom let go of a piece of my hair that she was about to wind around the barrel of a curling iron. We listened.

"Now," he said. "It's too late to rehearse all the songs."

This was it. Now it was coming. The lecture, the warnings, the what-were-you-thinkings. Well, I didn't need to hear it from Dad—I'd already been repeating it to myself, over and over, since I left the lemonade stand. If I had just listened to him earlier that afternoon, trusted that he knew what was best, we would have had all day to practice. Instead, I'd almost cost us the whole show, everything we had worked for. All because I trusted the wrong person. Myself.

But Dad surprised me again. He didn't lecture or scold. He didn't even raise his voice.

"It's too late to rehearse," he continued. "But that's all right. You have been rehearsing for months. For years. And you're ready." He took the old notebook out of his pocket. The set list. He flipped it open. Flipped and flipped.

To a blank page.

"What should we start with?"

None of us said a word. It seemed like a trick. I bit my thumbnail.

"Well? The three of you have been out there every day. You

171

know what the audience responds to. I want to hear what you have to say. I should have asked a long time ago." He looked from Ronnie to me to Junior. All of us looked away.

Dad picked up Junior's guitar and lifted the strap over his neck. He plucked the strings, quietly and lazily. "Verónica?"

She sat on the arm of my makeup chair and put her chin in her hand to think.

"Well, we've been playing 'Mi Ranchito' so long we hardly ever mess it up anymore. It's slow and easy." She plucked a cotton ball out of her makeup bag and tossed it at Junior when she said "slow."

"I *guess*," Junior said, flicking the cotton ball back at her. "I mean, if Verónica needs to start with something easy."

"Miranda?" Dad asked. "What do you think?" They all looked at me.

Ronnie was right. We'd been playing that song for years. Except it might have been too slow. Too easy. We only had three songs, after all. The first one needed to pull everyone out of their seats and onto their feet. That's what I thought. But I wasn't sure I could trust my own thoughts anymore, not when so much was at stake.

"She's right. We hardly ever mess up 'Mi Ranchito,'" I agreed. "We could start with that one."

Dad set the guitar on his lap to write "Mi Ranchito" on the first line of the notebook page. He looked up. "And Junior? The second song?"

Junior crossed one leg over the other and then back again. "What about 'My Girl'? They always eat it up when Randy sings 'My Girl.' They all sing along."

Mom started humming like she was trying to prove Junior's point.

"See?" he said.

They'd sing along, I thought, but they'd never know who we were. It was a fun song, but it wasn't *our* song.

"Any objections?" Dad asked. I opened my mouth to say something, but when I saw Ronnie nod her head, I closed my mouth and nodded my head too. If both of them thought it was a good idea, it probably was. What did I know?

Dad wrote it down and started playing again.

"Well, Miranda? Have you thought about the big finale?" He didn't look up from the guitar strings.

I didn't even have to think about it. "'El Rey,'" I said. "Like always."

Flor

(7:15 P.M.)

After dinner, I went out walking on the midway, then sat down to think behind the candy apple stand. Its green and white lights splashed bursts of color on the grass. I still had Randy's ball cap. It was sitting on one of my knees, almost like it was staring at me.

Accusing me.

I kicked it off. "She still had time to get back there if she wanted to, you know."

Probably. If she didn't get lost on the way. Or stuck in a crowd.

I didn't know why I cared. Or why I was defending myself to a hat.

I had done everything I could to save the zoo, and then everything I could to save the show.

The thing of it was, I did know why I cared. I cared because now the zoo *and* the show were in trouble, and I was out of ideas for saving anything.

It was darker. The sun was almost gone, just a warm orange glow like the wild poppies we sped past on the highway.

There was a sign taped to the booth where they had been selling cantaloupe milk shakes all day: SOLD OUT. In a few more hours, after the big main-stage show, the booths would close. The last of our customers would wobble to the exits with sunburned noses and blisters on their toes from walking around all day. The lights would blink out. When morning came, we would pack up all the rides, all the food stands, all the prizes, and all the fun and make our way to the next stop: San Joaquin County. Sixth grade.

"There you are." Mikey was still carrying around the pink gorilla. Only, he was holding it behind him now like he was giving it a piggyback ride. "Your dad's looking for you."

"I found him."

"So you know about the pig?"

"She's gone."

He dropped the gorilla and sat down next to me.

"Too bad you never got to try out that skateboard act. I was thinking, if Barsetti bought some big stuffed-animal pigs for prizes, I could carry around one of those and send people to the games *and* your show." He blew out through his lips. "But, Flor?" He hesitated. "Betabel was a mean pig."

I elbowed him. Softly, though. "She isn't mean. She just... was not where she belonged. She's going to a pig farm."

"Do you think she'll like it there?"

"Hope so."

"Maybe she'll make pig friends. If she isn't mean to them too."

I elbowed him again. Not as softly as the first time. "Don't you have somewhere to be? Aren't you supposed to be helping your brother?"

He ripped a clump of clover out of the ground and threw it. Little bits of dirt sprayed out behind so it looked like a tiny green comet.

"Nah. Some lady's about to break a record over at the Hoop Shoot. I can't get anyone to leave. Johnny's booth'll win next week, though. I can feel it." He patted the gorilla's head. "How'd *your* little plan work out? Where's Randy? Did you get her to eat the deep-fried pickles?"

Just about any way you looked at it—from upside down on the corkscrew coaster, or head-on in the bumper cars—my plan had not worked out very well. "She ate the pickles and she loved them. She's over at the main stage now. Or she should be."

"Without her lucky hat?" He pointed at the ball cap, still lying on the grass. "Ah." He nodded knowingly. "Did you steal it? Was that your plan? Sabotage?"

"I did not steal her hat."

I picked it up again. It was red with OUTLAWS embroidered on the front in swoopy white letters. The very front edge of the brim was worn thin from her pulling it down so much. Black plastic peeked through red threads.

It did not look very lucky, is what I'm saying.

But Randy hadn't said it was lucky. She'd said it reminded her of home and of how far she had come.

I had never played on a team before. Not baseball, not soccer, not anything. I used to think I would never belong.

But I belonged at Barsetti & Son, and that was sort of like a team. And teammates rooted for one another, looked out for one another.

I twirled the cap on my finger. Maybe I had come a long way too. Even if I had to leave the carnival, I would know I had friends here. I had more than I thought.

"Mikey, I need to borrow the gorilla."

Miranda

(7:35 P.M.—SHOWTIME)

I tapped out the beat with the toe of my boot.

Then with my hand against the side of my leg. *Bom, bom, bom, bom.* Junior's bass line was slow and easy.

I opened my eyes and sang.

There was a ripple of applause, like rain spattering on the windshield, as the audience recognized the song.

Their clapping should've been louder, though. I tried not to worry.

I pulled the microphone from its stand. I marched to one side of the stage, then over to the other. It wasn't the kind of song you tossed your hat to, really. Instead, when the notes were loud and lonesome, I touched the brim, bent my head back, and sang to the sky.

Another spatter of applause.

I looked over my shoulder at Ronnie. She mouthed slowly: *Keep going.*

I felt like the little girl at the livestock auction, waiting for someone to stand up, to raise their hand for me.

The grandstand wasn't full yet. Up there, people were still climbing to their seats, not paying us any attention at all.

I tried to ignore them because the crowd standing just below us was bigger than any we'd ever played for at the Family Side Stage.

Any we'd ever played for anywhere.

But they were not dancing.

Flor

(7:40 P.M.)

I'm sorry, baby. You know I'd let you in any other night, but Barsetti is in there, and if he sees I let you in without a wristband..." She looked at the line backed up behind me and smiled nervously.

"Angie, please. You have to let me through. Mr. Barsetti will never know it was you who let me in, and anyway, he won't catch me. I will only stay for Miranda's songs. Just three songs. *Please.*"

It was more because the line behind me kept growing longer and huffier than because she saw things my way, but Angie finally waved me through the turnstile.

"Flor, no! You can't bring that thing in there with you. You'll block someone's view!"

"Just three songs!" I called back.

I couldn't leave the gorilla behind. He was part of my new plan. My last-last chance.

Not to save the zoo.

Not even to save the show.

But to maybe save a friendship. To do the best with what I had.

Randy would not have been able to see me cheering for her in the crowd. She could barely see me when she was at the Family Side Stage.

But maybe she would see a giant pink gorilla if it was wearing her baseball cap.

I took a breath, lifted the gorilla high over my head, and plunged into the crowd. Randy and her brother and sister were playing one of those slow-swaying love songs again. People were singing along with them.

But it was a song like Grandpa listened to while he cleaned the truck. It didn't really sound like Randy's song, now that I had gotten to know her a little.

I couldn't see much of the stage, but between people's bobbing heads, I caught glimpses of rhinestones sparkling. With the gorilla on my shoulders, I pushed in closer.

Miranda

(7:45 P.M.)

Junior was right. They ate it up when I sang "My Girl." They were singing along.

Well, some of them were. The audience still seemed too far away from us.

Ronnie knew it. Junior knew it. He had slowly shuffled backward until he was playing not just behind me but behind Ronnie too. Her careful, quick fingers had stumbled over the keys like they almost never did.

I turned back to look at her again when the applause dwindled. She held up her index finger. One.

As in, *Just one more song?*

Or as in *one chance* and we were blowing it, just like Junior said?

Usually we could read one another's thoughts when we were onstage, but not tonight.

I wrapped both my hands around the microphone stand and held on like it was the only thing keeping me from sinking. And then I saw a flash of pink.

I whirled downstage and squinted into the audience. One of the faces below belonged to a giant pink gorilla. Mikey's pink gorilla, and he was wearing my baseball hat.

The gorilla, I mean. Not Mikey.

Only, Mikey wasn't the one carrying him. The gorilla was balanced on Flor's shoulders. She was jumping and waving, and she didn't care who was staring at her.

I smiled. Not a stage smile, but a crinkly-eyed real one. I pointed at Flor, and she pointed back.

That's when everything clicked.

Miranda y los Reyes had come a long way from our garage back at home, and we would go even further.

I still had friends. Maybe I couldn't make everyone like me, but some people did. They liked the real me.

I could trust myself. My plan was the right one.

"Thank you, Dinuba! We've had a great time with you this weekend. We have one more song tonight. It's a new one." I winked. "Rabbits love it, and I hope you do too."

I didn't wait for Ronnie. I let go of the microphone stand and clapped out the rhythm, just like we always practiced, only faster.

Junior shuffled over to me. He tapped the back of my arm with a tuning peg. No one else would've noticed it, but he was asking me a question.

"Yes," I answered. "Sí. I'm sure."

It was a song about hoping so hard your heart hurts and wondering what will happen next. And when it was over, the audience roared.

ACKNOWLEDGMENTS

To Jennifer Laughran, Nikki Garcia, Annie McDonnell, Sasha Illingworth, Angela Taldone, Erika Schwartz, and Elisabeth Ferrari: Thanks for making this book possible and so much better.

To the Great Central Valley—the Lodi Grape Festival, the Tracy Dry Bean Festival, the Ripon Almond Blossom Festival, the Linden Cherry Festival, the Manteca Pumpkin Fair, and especially the Stockton Asparagus Festival: Thanks for making room for us. Thanks for loving us back.

To David, Alice, and Soledad: Thanks for everything, always.

Turn the page for a preview of

Middle school drama is always on the menu.

STEF SOTO, Taco Queen

JENNIFER TORRES

AVAILABLE NOW

chapter
1

Papi had pretty much promised to stop bringing Tía Perla to Saint Scholastica School, but when the last bell rings on a Monday afternoon, there she is just the same, waiting for me in the parking lot: Tía Perla, yet again. Tía Perla, like always. Tía Perla, huffing and wheezing and looking a little bit grubby no matter how clean she actually is. Tía Perla, leaving anyone who comes near her smelling like jalapeños and cooking oil, a not-exactly-bad combination that clings to your hair and crawls under your fingernails. Tía Perla, Papi's taco truck, stuffed into a parking space meant for a much smaller car. A normal car. A station wagon! Something beige or black or white, with four doors and power windows.

I must look as annoyed as I feel because just then, my best friend, Amanda Garcia, stops explaining how she turned an old T-shirt into a new headband and wags her finger. "Watch it, Stef," she warns in her best scolding-abuelita voice. "Keep rolling your eyes like that, and they'll get stuck up there."

I roll my eyes at her so hard they almost bounce off my forehead. She snorts, pulls the headband over her ears, and jogs off to soccer practice, leaving me to deal with Papi and old Tía Perla on my own.

I didn't mind the taco truck when I was younger, and seeing Tía Perla in the parking lot of my Catholic school meant corn chips and cold soda for all my friends. Back then, when Papi lifted me up into her front seat, I was playground royalty. No one *else* got picked up in a taco truck.

But now hardly anyone else gets picked up *at all*, let alone in a taco truck.

I've been negotiating for months, trying to persuade Mami and Papi to let me walk alone—not even all the way home, just to the gas station a few blocks away from Saint Scholastica where Papi parks the truck most afternoons. I'd head straight there, I swore. Wouldn't stop for anything; wouldn't talk to anybody. I could tell they weren't crazy about the idea, but this weekend, Mami and Papi had finally given in.

So why was Tía Perla in the parking lot, with Papi in the front seat, waving?

I drop to the ground, pretending to tie my shoelace and thinking, Maybe if I'm down here long enough, Papi will remember our agreement, *leave*, and meet me at the gas station like we planned.

Instead, he honks the horn and waves even more wildly.

"Uh, isn't that your dad, Estefania?" Julia Sandoval asks, louder than she really needs to.

Just perfect. I stand up and gush, "Thank you, Julia. *So* much. You are *always. So. Helpful.*"

She just tilts her head and flashes her sparkling-sweet smile.

I walk across the parking lot, eyes glued to the ground and arms crossed sourly against my chest. I don't look up—not even when I'm climbing into the truck—until Papi asks, like he asks every single day, "Aprendiste algo?"

Did I *learn* something? That I can't trust him to keep his end of a deal, maybe. I keep my mouth shut while I sift furiously through my mental glossary of irritation, searching for words to tell him exactly how frustrated I am. Not coming up with any, I instead shoot Papi a glare that says, *Are you* kidding *me right now?* I hope that's clear enough.

His shoulders drop, and he shakes his head. "What can I tell you, m'ija? Those guys at the gas station must have forgotten their wallets or their appetites. Maybe both. I couldn't wait around for customers any longer. Let's see if they're hungry downtown." I don't know what to say to that, and before I can think of anything smart, I hear a *bam, bam, bam, bam* on my door.

"Huh?" I'm confused for a second, and then I realize who must be knocking. I crank down the window, and sure enough, it's Arthur Choi, all four feet ten inches of him—an even five feet with his hair included. He looks up at me and yanks his headphones down around his neck. They are bright orange and so big he looks almost like he's wearing a life preserver.

"Hey, Stef. Think I can get a ride to the library?" Usually, Arthur's mom picks him up from school, not because she doesn't trust him to walk alone, but because he lives so far away. When she has to work late, he goes to the library to wait for her, finishing his homework, reading his magazines, listening to his music. Without a chaperone. In peace. Arthur and I have known each other since kindergarten, back when his mom and my dad teamed up and trailed the school bus in her minivan anytime our class had a field trip. Unlike my parents, though, Arthur's seem to have noticed that he isn't five years old anymore.

I turn to Papi.

"Órale." He nods. It's a word that comes in many flavors. Sometimes it means "Yes," and other times "YES!"

Sometimes "Listen," and sometimes "I hear you."

This time it means "Of course!" and I slide to the middle of the bench seat as Arthur hops up next to me.

Finally, Papi starts the engine, and as soon as he does, his banda music comes bouncing out of the speakers and pouring—I'm sure of it—right through the open windows. Unfazed, Arthur bops his head right along to the *oompah-pah* rhythm. I slam mine back into the seat and squeeze my eyes shut.

"Please, can we just go now?"

chapter
2

Papi pulls over at the curb across from the library. I expect him to leave the truck running while Arthur grabs his back-pack off the floor of the cab, but instead, he parks, unbuckles his seat belt, and steps outside.

We can't be stopping here, I think, taking stock of the neighborhood on the other side of Tía Perla's windshield. No shoebox-shaped office buildings full of lawyers or accountants or real estate agents, their stomachs grumbling for a late-afternoon snack. No auto-repair shops with impatient walk-in customers looking for ways to kill time while they wait for their oil changes and smog checks. Nothing but neat houses with neat lawns, a basketball hoop in every other driveway.

Just behind the library, there's a small playground with a tire swing, a slide, and a couple of benches, and if you weren't an expert in taco truck terrain, you might consider it promising. But I know from experience that you could park for hours at a playground like that and be lucky to see even a dog walker or two. One of them might come up to the window, but just to ask for a free glass of water.

"Arturo," Papi calls.

Arthur lifts his nose out of his backpack, where he's been fishing for his library card. He squints at me, his scrunched-up eyebrows asking, *What's going on?*

"No idea," I say.

He opens his door, and we both climb down, following Papi's voice to the back of the truck. We find him at the cutting board, about to chop a bunch of green onions. Papi works quickly, dicing a tomato, sprinkling pepper. When he's finished, he presents Arthur with something that looks like a burrito, only it's wrapped in a giant lettuce leaf instead of a tortilla. "Prepared especially for you," he announces with a flourish. "The wheat-free, dairy-free, egg-free, nut-free, and meat-free super burrito."

Arthur is allergic to basically everything and is a vegetarian for environmental reasons. Sometimes, between customers, Papi experiments with new Arthur-friendly dishes, claiming the challenge keeps his kitchen skills as sharp as his knives. We add the best recipes to the Official Arthur Choi Menu, a note card taped to the door of the fridge. So far, there's a mango salad with charred corn and slivers of red onion; avocado halves stuffed with rice, green chili, cilantro, and bell peppers; and an almost-overripe banana, cut into coins and sautéed in margarine, brown sugar, and cinnamon until each crispy slice is floating in a rich, caramel-colored sauce.

I'm wondering what inspired this afternoon's lettuce-leaf burrito when I realize that if Papi had time to dream it up between customers, he really must have had a slow day with Tía Perla after all. *Aaaand* it's possible I overreacted about the whole gas station thing. I glance over at him. Papi looks up at me and winks before nudging Arthur to have a taste.

"Ándale," he says.

"Yeah, go on," I add, curious now. "Try it."

Arthur considers the burrito for a moment, then devours almost half of it in one enormous bite. Papi and I watch, hungry for his reaction.

"*Aww-oooohm*," he mumbles, cheeks puffed like they're hiding Ping-Pong balls. He swallows.

"Pretty good, Mr. Soto. Not as good as the bananas, but pretty good. Thanks."

"*Pretty* good?" Papi crosses his arms and cocks his head. "Pués, does it go on the menu?"

Arthur looks at me, looks at Papi, and grins.

"It goes on the menu."

"Órale!" Papi thunders, holding out his hands for Arthur and me to slap. "It goes on the menu. Specialty of the house."

As Arthur goes back to devouring his burrito, Papi locks Tía Perla's kitchen door and gives it a quick tap—the way you might congratulate an old friend with a pat on the back—then hops into the cab and settles into his seat.

Two bites later, when he's done eating, Arthur flashes me a peace sign and pulls on his earphones. Stick-straight tufts of spiky hair spring up around the orange band. "See ya," I say. Papi and I watch him cross the street. Not until the library doors part to let Arthur in, then close again safely behind him, does Papi start the truck.

"Vámonos?" he asks me.

"Let's go." I nod.

We drive to a convenience store downtown where the owner lets us use his parking lot as long as we send customers inside to buy their sodas. It's a fair deal. The little shop isn't the busiest stop on our route, but we know we can count on some regulars: commuters who pull in for tortas and tacos to tide them over on the drive home; gray-haired men in starched shirts who come to the store for lottery tickets and decide a burrito is a good bet, too.

While Papi lifts open the canopy, warms up the grill, and unfolds two steel chairs on either side of a salsa-stained card table, I drag my backpack to the spot at the cutting counter that he always leaves clear for me to finish my homework. He notices me sneaking a handful of corn chips, and before long, a quesadilla, cut into wedges and arranged around a dollop of chunky guacamole, appears on a plate next to my math book. People always ask if I get sick of taco truck food, if I'm bored eating the same thing night after night. But what they don't know is that it's never the same thing. Somehow Papi always prepares exactly what I'm craving. On the hottest days, when my bangs stick to my forehead, there are salads drizzled with lemon juice. When I leave school exhausted after a particularly tough history test, there's the comfort of a plain flour tortilla smeared with nothing but melting butter.

I spoon some guacamole onto my quesadilla and wonder what Mami's up to at home. Getting ready for work, I guess. She's a cashier at the open-all-night grocery store. You would never believe, she always says, what people need at one o'clock in the morning: a box of pancake mix, a birthday card, a cantaloupe. Most of the time, she doesn't get home until I'm already in bed, and since Mami and Papi won't even *think* about letting me stay home alone, I'm parked with Tía Perla until the dinner rush lets up—it feels like forever.

Finally, though, Papi taps me on the shoulder. He has scooped the last glob of sour cream onto the last super burrito of the day, and it's time to pack up Tía Perla. We take her to the commissary, where drivers from all over the city store their supplies and keep their food trucks overnight. I help him wipe down the countertops and rinse out the big plastic containers we use for storing onions and tomatoes. When we're finished, he tucks my backpack under his arm, and we walk together to our pickup. The lights in the parking lot blaze bright white against the inky sky. I'm wondering how I could re-create the effect with paint and paper when Papi jokes, "Say buenas noches to Tía Perla." I yawn and wave—she looks a little out of place parked next to so many other trucks with flashier paint jobs and shinier chrome bumpers, her tired headlights pleading with us not to leave her behind.

David Siders

Jennifer Torres

is an award-winning writer and the author of *The Fresh New Face of Griselda*; *Flor and Miranda Steal the Show*; *Stef Soto, Taco Queen*; and *Finding the Music/En pos de la música*. A former journalist, she is inspired by her Mexican-American heritage. She lives with her family in Southern California. You can visit her online at jenntorres.com.

LAUGH OUT LOUD with a HEARTWARMING STORY by

JENNIFER TORRES